SNOWBOUND REUNION

BY

BARBARA McMAHON

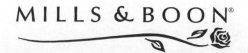

MILLS & BOON®

First published in Great Britain 2006
Large Print edition 2007
Harlequin Mills & Boon Limited,
Eton House, 18-24 Paradise Road,
Richmond, Surrey TW9 1SR

© Barbara McMahon 2006

ISBN-13: 978 0 263 19437 1
ISBN-10:   0 263 19437 X

Set in Times Roman 16¾ on 20 pt.
16-0307-46908

Printed and bound in Great Britain
by Antony Rowe Ltd, Chippenham, Wiltshire

CHAPTER ONE

CATH MORGAN drove through the Virginia countryside anxious to reach her destination. She ignored the stand of trees lining the road, raising their barren branches to the winter sky. It was a beautiful day, cold and sunny. She should have been enjoying the scenery, but heartache was her companion and she never gave a thought to anything but reaching the house at the end of the journey. Sanctuary. The place she had loved as a child, and wanted to escape to now that things were unraveling.

She'd left Washington, D.C., that morning, after months of soul searching. It wasn't easy walking out on a marriage. But for a woman married six years, it had not been as hard as she had expected. Out of all that time, her husband had only been home a total of one year, seven months, two weeks and three days. She'd counted it up.

She'd spent two summers in Europe, to be closer to where Jake was. But even then, he'd rarely been able to spend more than a few days with her.

What kind of marriage was that? For all intents and purposes she was a single person unable to have a normal social life because of a legal tie to a man half a world away.

Time to change all that.

She felt as if she were cutting a part of herself out with a dull knife.

Cath noted on the highway sign flashing by that she was drawing closer to her turnoff. The exit that would take her to the house her aunt Sally had left to her when she died last summer.

Jake had come home for the funeral. That had added the three days to the tally. But then he'd left. She hadn't wanted him to go, had begged him to stay, but some skirmish captured the world's attention, and he went to report it.

Aunt Sally's death had been the catalyst for this change. She had been Cath's last living relative. There was no one else. If Cath wanted children to live on after her, she had to do something about it.

She'd talked to Jake several times on the phone, e-mailed him almost daily—at least at first. But he didn't want to discuss things long distance. And would not return home.

Cath gripped the wheel tighter. She wasn't going to think about the past. For far too long she'd put her life on hold for Jake Morgan. Now she was taking it back.

She'd known when she married him that he was a reporter with a travel lust that took him all over the globe. From armed skirmishes to natural disasters, Jake Morgan always sought to be in the middle of the next late breaking news. It had been exciting in those first months to be a part of his life, to tell friends and co-workers that her husband was Jake Morgan.

E-mail and phone calls had kept them connected. And she'd been thrilled each time he came home, hoping that this was the time he'd stay. Her summer in Athens and the one in Rome had seemed romantic at first. But she was as lonely there as at home, and didn't speak either language.

After six years, she was tired of their electronic relationship. She was tired of constant disappointments. She wanted a husband at home every night, someone to eat dinner with and discuss their respective days. Someone to share child raising with. Someone to give her the baby she longed for. Someone to grow old with.

Jake was not that man. The realization had come slow and hard. But she'd admitted it finally. And taken steps to change the status quo.

She recognized her exit approaching and slowed to turn off the highway onto a quiet country road. It soon narrowed and twisted as it meandered through the wooded area. Historic Williamsburg was not too far from the house on the James River that had once been her aunt's. Cath's parents had died of influenza when a particular virulent strain had swept through the country the winter of her senior year in college. Her mother's parents had been dead before she was born, her father's dying within months of each other when she was still a young child. Her birth had been a surprise to everyone, occurring when her parents were in their forties and had long given up any hope for a baby.

Cath began to recognize familiar landmarks. She smiled sadly as she rounded the last bend and saw the old house in solitary splendor on the banks of the historic river. She'd spent many summers here with her aunt. Even knowing Aunt Sally had died last summer, Cath halfway expected to find her peering through the windows, watching for her arrival.

She turned onto the dirt driveway, heading past the house toward the old carriage house in back. For a moment her imagination flickered to the past. The house had been built in the 1770s, had withstood the war for American independence, and then the bloody Civil War that almost tore the country asunder ninety years later. The clapboard structure had been renovated a time or two. The plumbing wasn't the best in the world, but sufficed. Electricity had been added long ago and probably needed to be updated to accommodate all the modern electric devices.

Cath wasn't sure if she'd be the one to handle that. One of the reasons for her visit was to decide what to do about the place.

She stopped near the back door and shut off the engine, looking around her. The grass lay dying in the winter sun, long and shaggy. She'd tried to get a caretaker for the grounds, but dealing with a firm long distance wasn't the easiest way to handle things, and it looked as if they had neglected the job.

Cath thought she'd best sell it and get from under the responsibility. Yet every once in a while, she daydreamed about moving to Williamsburg and living in the old house.

She hadn't voiced that option to anyone, but it rose higher on her list of things to think about. She was a great teacher and would have no trouble finding a job wherever she went. Maybe a clean break from everything would be best. If she moved here, she'd have a place to live in that wouldn't have a single memory of Jake.

She planned to spend her entire school break working on the house—and considering her options. Sadly she was doing it alone.

Her aunt had been a spinster, never married. She'd loved Cath's visits and always made sure they toured Historic Williamsburg each summer and went many times to the beach. Cath remembered most fondly the lazy days lying in the grass in the backyard beneath the weeping willow tree, on the banks of the river, watching the water drift by. The trees had been in full leaf every summer, providing plenty of dapple shade in the hot Virginia summer. They looked bare and bleak without their leafy canopy.

Everything looked a little bleak in winter, reflecting the way she felt.

She and Jake had only managed one Christmas together, their second. Other years she had spent part of the day with her friend Abby and Abby's family. She'd been invited again this year, but Cath had wanted to spend it in the old house. She needed to get used to doing things by herself if she was serious about ending her marriage.

She climbed out of the car, studying the old, two-story clapboard house. It had been around for a couple of hundred years and Cath expected it would survive another couple of hundred.

She'd tried to keep up her spirits the last weeks of the school term. There was no sense letting anyone else know how difficult the last few months had been. Once her decision had been made, Cath thought it would become easier. It was not proving so. Her heart ached in longing and wishful thinking. But she was determined to see the change through, and make a different kind of life for herself in the future.

Cath had wished she could be a part of a large family when she'd been a child. But she'd been the only child of older parents. Her desire for siblings had faded as she grew up. And she found lots of joy in teaching her third-grade class every year.

But this year, with the death of Aunt Sally, the desire for children of her own had escalated. She'd tried to talk to Jake about it, but he'd pooh-poohed the idea, saying their lives were full the way they were.

His maybe, not so hers.

Others spent weeks shopping for Christmas, making cookies and pies and decorating their homes. She had finished her short list before Thanksgiving. And there wasn't much reason to decorate their condo when she was the only one there.

She needed to get this place sorted out and packed up. If not now, then it would have to wait until summer. That was a long time for the house to remain empty. She wondered what it would be like filled with childish laughter, the sound of running feet and shrieks of delight.

She drew a deep breath. She wasn't out of love with Jake, but she couldn't stay in a marriage that existed more on paper than in reality. One day she hoped to make a happy life with someone else. Once she got over Jake. If she ever did.

Opening the car door, she caught her breath at the cold air. Time to get inside and see about warming up the big old house before bedtime. There was plenty to do and not as much time as she wished to do it all. Could she have the place ready for sale by January first? The project gave her something to focus on. She would hardly notice another holiday was passing without her husband.

Her e-mails over the last several weeks had urged him to return home. Jake had always said things were too hot to leave. She tried to explain her unhappiness and the decision she was making, but couldn't come right out and tell him via e-mail. She wanted to tell him in person.

If he didn't return home, soon, however, she wasn't sure what she'd do. She'd have to write him, not let him find out from an attorney. She'd even written a practice note and left it at home. Not that she expected him to show up. It was more important to Jake to report the news from some hot spot than spend the holidays with his wife. She'd have to write him in January, when she returned home.

She had to tell him their marriage was over.

Tears filled her eyes. She dashed them away, blaming them on the cold wind. Time to get inside and warm up.

Jake Morgan let himself into the town house. He was exhausted. The flight home had been one delay and mishap after another. He should be thankful the plane hadn't crashed, but that was about the only holdup he hadn't experienced.

Maybe it had been a sign he wasn't supposed to come home for Christmas. But Cath's e-mails lately had been disturbing. She'd almost demanded he come home. She rarely even asked. Plus, he wanted to see her. His flying visit in August had been solely to attend her aunt's funeral. Not enough time to spend together beyond the duties of that sad event.

"Cath?" he called.

The place was silent. Jake headed for the bedroom. A quick shower, a nap and he'd be good to go. She must be out shopping. He knew school was out for the Christmas holidays, so she wasn't at work.

Maybe she was visiting her friend Abby. They could be baking Christmas cookies with Abby's kids. Cath always liked the season. Her notes were usually full of decorating at the school she'd done, or the treats she baked for colleagues.

The house felt cold and lonely with her absence.

He glanced into the living room as he passed,

stopped by the envelope propped on the mantel, his name in large print.

A sickening dread took hold. His instincts had been honed by years of dangerous assignments. He knew better than to ignore them.

Dropping his duffel bag, he crossed the expansive living room and picked up the envelope. He ripped it open and stared at the words for endless moments. He crushed the letter, the words almost unfathomable—she wanted to end their marriage.

Cath had left him. She was gone. The house was empty and lifeless for a reason—the heart of it had gone.

Jake reread the words, as if doing so could change them. They remained the same, indelibly engraved in his mind. He felt sick. Disbelief warred with the words dancing before his eyes.

The woman he loved beyond all else had not loved him enough to stay.

Crushing the paper in his hand he turned, as if seeking her.

It was his fault, and he knew it. He'd deliberately stayed away this fall as if sensing the change in her, fearing this very thing. Why had he thought she wouldn't take such a step unless consulting him first? So they could *talk*. She always wanted to talk about things, nitpick them to death. She'd given enough hints all fall that he should have picked up on them. Subconsciously maybe he had. Why else change his plans at the last moment and return home for Christmas?

But he was home now, dammit. Where was Cath?

He ran up the stairs to their bedroom. Throwing open the closet door, he breathed a sigh of relief when he saw most of her clothes. She hadn't moved out. Not yet, at least.

Her suitcase was gone.

He went into the bathroom, assessing what was there and what was not. She'd gone somewhere for Christmas, she was coming back. He could wait.

Jake shook his head and turned. He was not

going to sit around while Cath ended their marriage. He wanted to set her straight on that. Only he had to find her first.

Walking slowly downstairs, he tried to think. He was known for his coolness under fire, why couldn't he think now?

Abby would know. She was Cath's best friend.

It took a few moments to locate Cath's address book. Jake looked around the condo with impatience. It was his home, too. Just because he wasn't often here didn't mean he should feel like a stranger in his own home. He dialed Abby's number.

"Hello?"

"Abby?"

"Yes?"

"Jake Morgan here. Do you know where Cath is?"

"Where are you?"

"Home."

"She said you weren't coming home for the holidays."

"I planned to surprise her. Only she got the first surprise in."

"What do you mean?" Abby's voice was cautious.

"A letter."

There was silence on the other end.

"Where is she, Abby?"

"She says it's over, Jake. She's been agonizing over this all fall. Let her go."

"Like hell, I will. Where is she?"

"If she wanted you to know, she'd have left word. I can't help you, Jake."

She hung up.

Jake swore and slammed down the phone.

If she had not expected him home, Cath wouldn't have gone to stay at Abby's. They could drive over to each other's place in less than ten minutes. It meant she went somewhere else. But where?

Aunt Sally's house.

Her refuge, she'd once said.

He scooped up his duffel and headed out. A bath

and sleep would have to wait. He needed to find his wife and talk her out of her plans to leave.

Cath finished the makeshift meal and cleared the kitchen. She still wore her jacket, the house was too cold to take it off. The old furnace had been difficult to start, but she'd finally managed. Now it was just a question of time before the coldness was dispelled.

She'd made up the bed in the room she'd always used. Aunt Sally's room was larger, but Cath wasn't ready to make that step yet. She wished her aunt had electric blankets. Something was needed to warm the bed if she wanted to sleep in it tonight. Maybe she could use the old-fashioned bed warming pan that had hung in the cellar for as long as Cath could remember. Her aunt had told her how generations of Williamsons had used it to warm their beds before retiring. Long before central heating kept the house a comfortable temperature.

Tonight Cath knew how the early settlers felt.

She didn't think she could take off her clothes to get into her nightgown without freezing. But she hesitated before going down in the dark old cellar. She didn't like going there in daylight, she really didn't want to go now, warming pan or not. Plus, she wasn't sure she knew how to use one

The warm water felt good on her hands as she washed the few dishes. She'd found the pilot light had remained on for the hot water heater, so she had instant hot water. Maybe she should take a bath. Wasn't there a small space heater in the bathroom? Aunt Sally hated to turn on the big furnace before it was needed, as she put it. She'd delayed the lighting of the furnace until way down in the fall, using the space heater in the bathroom, and letting the sunshine streaming in through tall windows warm the ambient temperature through the house during the day.

Cath wasn't as stouthearted. She liked comforts—at least heat and lights.

She'd brought some books to read, and considered heading for bed now just to get beneath the covers. But it was only seven-thirty—too early to go to bed.

Cath had dusted and vacuumed the main rooms downstairs, and cleaned the one bathroom and her bedroom since her arrival. Giving all a lick and a promise, as her aunt used to say. Too much to do in one day, but she had two weeks ahead of her. She was tired, still cold and lonely. She wished… No, don't go there. A good night's sleep would be just the thing. In the morning she'd start cleaning and clearing in the back bedroom and work her way through the second story and then the first to clear clutter and decide what to do with Aunt Sally's furnishings and mementos. Her clothing had been donated last summer. But there were still generations of things in the house to sort, if she included every-thing stored in the cellar.

She'd leave the cellar for last. No telling what was down there. It was dark, with faint illumi-nation, and piles of boxes, trunks and old furni-ture. As a child, she'd found it spooky. The door often slammed shut, apparently for no reason. Aunt Sally said it contained the remnants of all the families who had lived in the house.

Cath had asked about ghosts when she'd been little. Nothing to be afraid of, her aunt assured her, just gentle reminders of ancestors long gone. Cath was not looking forward to that clearing job.

She checked the locks on the front door before going up to her bedroom. A sweep of headlights came in through the beveled glass. She stared at the driveway. Was someone lost and asking directions? Or was it a neighbor who had seen the lights and wanted to know who was in Sally Williamson's house?

The beveled glass distorted the man who got out of the car. He reached in for a bag and slammed the door. The night wasn't completely black. She could still make him out from the faint starlight, striding toward the house. He might not be clearly visible in the darkness, but she'd recognize that stride anywhere. It was Jake.

Her heart skipped a beat, then raced. For a split second, gladness filled her—then dismay. What was he doing here? Why hadn't he told her he was coming home for the holidays? How had he found her?

She stepped back from the door, to one side, out of sight, wanting to run to her bedroom and hide beneath the covers. Instead, like a deer caught in headlights, she watched as he approached the door. She hadn't seen him since last August. He e-mailed as regularly as he could, complaining if she didn't write to him often. But there wasn't as much to share as there used to be. And once she began thinking about leaving, she had found it difficult to communicate as if everything was fine.

He knocked on the door.

Do or die time, Cath thought. Why had Jake come? Surely he'd seen the letter she'd left just in case he arrived at home.

She opened the door a crack, standing slightly behind it. The cold air swept in.

"Hi, Jake. I didn't expect you."

He pushed gently and stepped inside, dumping the bag and glaring at her.

"What the hell kind of letter was that you left?"

"An explanatory one," she said. "I thought if you showed up and I wasn't there, you might worry."

"But not worry about your leaving me?"

"I'm safe."

"That's not the point and you know it," he said. "I busted my butt to get home for the holidays and you weren't even there. Instead I get some damn-fool letter saying you're calling it quits."

"That's right," she said evenly. She could do this. She just had to ignore the spark of feelings that flared at the sight of him. All the pain of her decision, the regrets and might-have-beens sprung up. She pushed the thoughts away.

He looked drawn and tired. There was a two-day's growth of beard on his cheeks and chin, and his eyes were bloodshot and weary-looking.

His clothes were rumpled. Despite it all, her heart called out, unhappy with her choice.

"I didn't come all this way, through the worst connection of flights I think I've ever taken, to be dumped. I've come home to my wife," Jake said, reaching out, pulling her into his arms and kissing her.

CHAPTER TWO

CATH resisted as long as she could, but his kisses always drove her wild. Despite her best intentions, she returned the kiss, reveling in the feel of the man holding her. It had been too long. She had missed him so much! She loved being held by him, being kissed. She felt alive, whole, complete. Why couldn't it always be like this?

Then reality returned. Common sense took over and slowly she pushed against his embrace. They'd always been terrific together in a physical sense. But it wasn't enough. No longer.

She couldn't stay married to Jake Morgan. She wanted more than to be a part-time wife. She deserved more!

She pushed harder and he released her.

Breathing fast, he looked at her, his gaze intense and assessing.

"Nice of you to stop by," Cath said, opening the door. "Have a nice holiday."

He reached around her and slammed it shut. "I'm staying, get used to the idea."

"You can't stay here. I'm leaving you."

"So leave."

"This is my house. You leave."

Cath realized they were starting to sound like four-year-olds. She didn't need this.

"Not tonight. I've been up for more than twenty-four hours. I had planned to get some sleep this afternoon, but instead had to drive down here," he said, looking around.

"No one invited you," she said, glaring at him.

"I invited myself. It's cold in here."

"The heater's on, it was freezing before. It'll take a while to warm the entire house. You could have told me you were coming home. I asked you often enough in the past weeks."

"I didn't know for sure if I could make it and

I didn't want to get your hopes up. No worries there, I guess," he said.

"We could have had this discussion in Washington if I'd known you were coming. I could have come down after talking with you," Cath said. She didn't want him to stay. She was too afraid her carefully constructed rationale would crumble around him. But it was late and he looked exhausted. Could he find a motel room in town? Williamsburg was bursting at the seams with all the tourists who came for the holidays. Most places had been booked solid months ago.

"We definitely need to discuss things, but not tonight. Where are we sleeping?" he asked.

"*I'm* sleeping in my old room. If you insist on staying, you can have Aunt Sally's room. I'm not sleeping with you. You read the letter, I'm calling it quits, Jake." For a moment, she hoped he'd sweep away all the points leading to her decision. But he picked up his duffel and started for the stairs.

"We'll talk in the morning. Isn't that what you like to do, talk things to death?" he asked

"Not this time," Cath said quietly. She had no words left. No hope.

Jake paused at the bottom of the stairs and looked back at her. In two strides he crossed the short distance, leaning over to kiss her. She clenched her hands into tight fists, resisting with all she was worth.

"We're not over, Cath," he said.

She watched as he climbed the stairs, her heart pounding. The wooden floors echoed his steps. She could trace his location by the sounds. He paused at her room then moved on down the hall to the next one. A breath escaped, she hadn't known she was holding. None of the other beds were made, he'd have to fend for himself. And leave in the morning. Tears threatened. His being here would make everything that much harder.

Cath couldn't believe Jake had shown up out of the blue. Nothing in his recent e-mails had even hinted he was thinking of coming home.

The last she'd heard, he was someplace in the Middle East.

She hugged herself against the chill, and not just the temperature in the room. She couldn't go to bed now, her thoughts were a total mishmash, spinning and jangled.

His kiss had been all she could have ever hoped for. He could always make her feel like the queen of the world with one kiss.

But the important things—discussions of their future together, planning their family—he always sidestepped, only saying they'd deal with whatever fate decreed. She wasn't going to go along with that anymore. She wanted her freedom from this marriage, wanted to be able to forge new ties eventually, and even try for a baby. And she didn't plan to wait until she was in her forties as her parents had been!

It was late when Cath finally went upstairs. She had paced the living room until she couldn't stand it, exquisitely aware that Jake was asleep upstairs. She was halfway tempted to wake him up and have that discussion now. She'd been a long, agonizing time coming to this decision. She just hoped Jake accepted it with some grace.

But she was not going to wake him up. She'd be civilized and wait until morning. The house had warmed enough she was willing to try changing into her nightgown, glad she'd brought the long flannel one with rosebuds and pink ribbons. She needed the high neck, long sleeves and long length to keep her warm. And to keep from thinking romantic thoughts about her husband.

Sleep was the farthest thing from her mind, however, when she did get into bed. All she could think about was Jake in a room down the hall. She hoped he wasn't going to be difficult about this. He ought to be glad she'd started the ball rolling. He was never home. This way, he never even had to fly back to the U.S. between assignments. He could flit off to whatever late-breaking news spot drew him without any cares in the world.

Somehow she knew he wasn't seeing it quite that way.

When Cath awoke the next morning, she immediately thought about Jake. His being here was a complication she didn't need or expect. Why had he returned? He hadn't made it home for the last four Christmases, why this one? Had her pleas in her e-mails finally made a dent? Or was he planning another brief stay like last August? She knew better than to get her hopes up. Six years of living on the periphery of Jake Morgan's life had taught her well.

Dressing rapidly in the large bathroom, she became convinced her aunt Sally had been of far sturdier stock than she. It was still cold enough to show her breath and Cath didn't like it one bit. She'd have to see about turning the heater higher. The small space heater wasn't up to the task of dispelling the chill.

Once dressed, she went downstairs without hearing any sound from Jake's room. He'd looked exhausted last night. If he'd been up for more than twenty-four hours, then maybe he'd sleep in late.

Or at least late enough to enable her to get her prioritics straight and her ducks in a row. He'd want an explanation, she'd give him one—logically and calmly. He could rant and rave all he wanted, but her mind was made up. She just hoped she could keep from descending into a rant herself. She'd kept a lot of her disappointments and anger inside. Only lately had she allowed herself to admit to all the things wrong with their union. It wouldn't be fair to dump them on Jake all at once. She should have told him all along how she resented the time he spent away from her. How lonely she had been for years.

Looking into the empty refrigerator, Cath wondered what to do for breakfast. She'd originally planned to eat at one of the cafés in town and then go grocery shopping. Maybe she should follow through with her plan, no telling how long Jake would sleep. And if he did waken before she returned, it might show him she was serious about their ending their marriage. In the past she would have stayed to prepare him breakfast. Today he was on his own.

It was after eleven when Cath returned. The minute she opened the kitchen door, she knew Jake was up. The fragrance of fresh coffee filled the kitchen. Where had he unearthed that old percolator of her aunt's? And the coffee to go with it? She'd made do with instant yesterday when she'd arrived.

Cath placed two grocery bags on the counter and turned to get the rest.

"I'll help," Jake said, coming into the kitchen from the hall.

She shook her head. "No need, I can manage." She wasn't giving in an inch.

Jake ignored her, however, and followed her to the car, reaching in the trunk to withdraw two more bags. Cath took the last one and closed the trunk.

"I said I could manage," she said, following his longer stride to the house.

"I'm sure you can, but why not take help when it's offered?" he asked reasonably.

She placed her bag on the table and shrugged out of her coat. Did he realize how much she didn't want him there? Jake had always had a stubborn streak. Now was not the time for it to take hold.

Putting the things away, Cath geared herself up for the coming confrontation. She had to stay calm, she told herself over and over. Not let Jake rile her or make her angry or talk her out of her decision. She'd tried not to look at him, not wanting to worry that he looked almost gaunt and tired beyond belief.

She'd thought everything through all fall long. She would be rational and certain.

She looked across the room. Jake leaned against the counter, legs crossed at the ankles, arms crossed over his chest, his gaze steady-focused on her.

"Want to tell me what this is all about?" he asked.

She put the cans of corn and beans in the cupboard. "I thought the letter said it all. I'm ending our marriage." She almost smiled in relief at how calm she sounded, but she didn't feel like smiling. She felt like crying.

"Why?"

No outburst, no denial, just one quiet word.

Cath turned to him, taking a deep breath. Do or die time. "Our marriage is not working for me. I want more than what we have. This is nothing new. We've argued about the entire setup more than once. I say what I want, you say things that sound placating, then take off for another five months to someplace I've never heard of until it's so common on the nightly news it becomes part of everyday life. I worry about you, but you don't seem to worry about me. I want a family, you don't. Jake, there are dozens of reasons to end this. I can't think of one to keep on the way we've been."

"How about love?"

"What about it? Do you love me? You have a funny way of showing it. I think you're comfortable with me. You like having me in D.C. to keep a place for you to return to when you get stateside. But how much of a relationship do we really have? Do I know any of your co-workers? Do you know any of mine? What was I most worried about this fall? What was your happiest moment last month? We don't know any of that, because we aren't really a couple. We're two people bound by a marriage license, who don't even live in the same country most of the time."

Jake didn't say a word. Cath had thought about this long and hard and she wasn't going to make it easier for him. Her nerves shook, but she continued to put up the groceries. Sooner or later he'd say something. She was not going to be the first to break the silence. Not this time.

"You knew what my job was like before we were married," he said at last.

"Yes and no," she replied. She knew this would be one argument. "I knew you worked for an international news bureau. But I had no idea of the reality of that. I didn't know until we lived it that you would be gone more than you're home. That I'd be so lonely and yet unable to do much about it. I certainly didn't know that when I was ready to think about a family, you wouldn't be as excited to start as I was."

"We never talked about having kids."

"Aunt Sally's death shook me up, more than I suspected at first. I want to have a family, be connected to others on the planet. We're not getting any younger. I don't want to be old like my parents were."

"I thought we wanted the same thing—living in the capital, having friends, doing things—"

"That's just it, Jake, we don't. Not together. We went to a concert at the Kennedy Center five years ago. Five years. Other than that, if I want to see a play or concert, I have to get Abby or another friend to go with me. What kind of marriage is that?"

His jaw clenched. Cath could tell he was keeping a tight leash on his emotions. Maybe, once, she'd like to see that leash slip. To really know what he was feeling. But Jake was too good a reporter to insert his feelings into things. Maybe that was part of the problem; she never felt he was totally involved, but was always observing. Or getting ready to make a commentary.

"Maybe there's room for improvement, but you don't just throw away six years of marriage without trying to save it," he countered.

"If you wanted this to work, you needed to do something before now. I haven't gone anywhere. What do you suggest, quitting your job? I don't see that. And if you don't, you won't be home nights, so we're in the same loop as always."

She folded the grocery bags, stuffed them in a cupboard and turned to leave, her knees feeling weak, her heart racing, tears on the verge. But she'd done it. She'd maintained a cool facade. He'd never know how sick she felt inside, how her heart was truly breaking.

It was pointless to argue. Nothing was going to change. Her mind was made up. One day he'd admit she'd been right. She hoped she herself felt that way!

"Wait, Cath. I'll admit maybe things have been in a rut lately. But this is my career we're talking about. It takes me where the news is. I can't say I'll stay in D.C. and only report on what's happening in Washington."

She paused at the doorway and looked back at him. "It's more than a job, or even a career, it's your life, Jake. Face it. You love the adrenaline rush of plunging into a war zone, or daring mother nature when faced with catastrophes. A job is something you go to for a few hours a day and then go home and have a real life."

"Someone has to report the news, Cath."

"I'm not arguing that, I'm just saying I don't want to be the person contributing to it by giving up my husband. I want a man I can rely on to be there for me."

"I'm only a phone call away."

"How long did it take you to get back this trip? You said you'd been up more than twenty-four hours. You may be a phone call away, but it took you a long time to physically get back. What if there'd been an emergency? What if I really needed you?"

"What if you do in the future? I won't be there if we get divorced."

Cath stared at him for a moment. "I want to get married again."

Jake looked dumbfounded. Then anger flared. "Your letter said there wasn't another man."

"There's not, where would I meet someone? There's no one now, that's the truth. But I hope to find someone, a man who wants the same things I do—especially children. I feel I've wasted six years of my life hoping you'd want what I want and we could start a family. It's never going to happen, is it, Jake? You'll always have a dozen excuses and then be off to Beirut or Singapore."

"You and I need to work on things a bit more, maybe. No, wait." He held up a hand when she started to speak. "No maybe about it. I see where you're coming from. I can try to meet you partway, Cath, but to just chuck everything after all these years doesn't make sense."

"Only because you're just hearing about it now. I've been thinking about this since you left last August. I wasn't ready to be alone after Aunt Sally died. She was my last relative."

"I'm a relative. I'm your husband."

"I'm talking blood kin and you know it. I felt absolutely alone in the world. I needed you and you took off."

"I didn't realize that," he said slowly.

"I came to that conclusion several weeks later," she said, smiling sadly. "It's because you don't really know me anymore. I'm not the twenty-two-year-old, excited to be falling in love with a man of the world. I'm a responsible adult who has really been living on her own for most of the six years of our marriage. I've grown up. My goals and dreams have changed. I've changed."

Jake studied her a long moment. "Maybe I have as well."

"Maybe, but I wouldn't know, would I?"

"I don't want a divorce."

"It's not all about you anymore, Jake."

He looked startled at that. "It was never just about me," he said.

"Yes, it has been, but no more. I've made up my mind to take back my life and make it like I want."

Cath turned and walked down the hall to the stairs. She'd planned to start cleaning the upstairs bedrooms today. She only had four days until Christmas, and then a week after that before she had to return to Washington. If she did one room a day, she'd be finished on time. She had to focus on that and not what might have been.

Jake followed her. "Cath, that kiss last night should have told you something," he said.

She paused midway up the steps, holding on to

the banister as she turned to look at him. "Sure, sex between us has always been great. But there's more to marriage than sex a few times a year. Don't you get it, Jake, it's over. I'm moving on. You can do what you want. Preferably from Washington. I think you should leave."

"We're not divorced yet, Cath. I'm staying."

Cath wanted to yell at him that she didn't want him around, that his mere proximity was disturbing, giving her ideas she had no business entertaining. She'd loved him so much, why couldn't he have seen that and offered more than what they'd shared? She needed to keep her goal firm and not be swayed by the dynamic presence of the man or her lost dreams.

"I don't want you to stay," she said.

"I don't want to leave. I don't think you can physically remove me."

Cath shook her head in frustration. "Of course not. Stay if you wish. Just keep out of my way."

"What are you doing here anyway? Running

from Washington?" he asked, ignoring her last comment.

"I'm planning to sort through things. See what the house needs to fix it up. I'm not sure what I want to do with it." She started to turn back up the stairs, but continued to look at him over her shoulder. "I may move here and get a job locally." How would he like that bit of news?

Jake scowled and began to climb the stairs. Cath didn't exactly run the rest of the way up, but she wanted to make sure she was firmly on the second floor before he could crowd her on the steps, or touch her. Or kiss her again. She needed to make sure there was none of that to muddle her thinking, or give her ideas that would fizzle to nothing as soon as the call of adventure summoned him back.

For a moment Cath felt a pain that almost doubled her over. She had loved Jake so much, had such high plans for their lives together. And it had come to this. Trying to be civil a week before Christmas. Tears threatened again.

"Can I help?" he asked.

"You should get started if you want to get to Washington before dark," she said.

"I'm staying, Cath. If you're serious about going through with a divorce, this will be our last Christmas together."

"Or second one, depending on how you look at it."

Jake sighed. "You're right and I'm sorry. I should have been home for Christmas every year."

"That surprises me to hear. You've never been sentimental. Why the change of heart?"

"Getting older, I guess. Doesn't everyone make decisions they later regret? I regret not spending more time with you. Especially in light of what you've just said. Don't you know the thought of you at home kept me going when times got rough?"

Cath had a boatload of regrets—that things had turned out the way they had, that she had spent so many lonely years wishing Jake had been with her watching TV together instead of her watching alone for glimpses of him. Wishing she'd shared more of her dreams with him. The biggest regret was that they'd not had any children. She could have stood the empty nights better if she'd had someone to lavish her love upon.

She stepped into the back bedroom. The curtains were dusty and closed. She pulled them open, dislodging a cascade of dust while letting in the cold winter light.

"I wish I could open the window to clear the air, but I had enough cold yesterday," she said, surveying the furnishing.

"Do you know anything about antiques?" Jake asked, stepping close enough beside her she could feel the radiant heat from his body.

"Not much. But I can recognize good quality furnishings. I'm only keeping things I like. I thought I'd ask a couple of antique dealers to come and give me an estimate on what things are worth." Hoping he wouldn't notice, she stepped to the side, putting a bit more distance between them.

"Tell them you're doing it for insurance purposes, you'll get a better reading," he suggested, stepping farther into the room and trailing a finger across a dusty table.

"Good idea. Good grief, where do I start?"

"With a vacuum and dust cloth. I'll help."

Cath tilted her head slightly. "You'll be late getting off for Washington."

He looked at her and grinned, the expression causing her heart to skip a beat. "I'm not going back to Washington without you. You might as well make up your mind to that. So I guess I'm here until the new year. Where are the dust cloths?"

Cath gave in. If the news bureau called, he'd be gone in a heartbeat. And she could use some help if other rooms looked like this one.

"Just as long as there's no misunderstanding," she cautioned.

"I'm clear on everything you've said," he replied, amusement lurking in his gaze. "But that doesn't mean I won't try to change your mind."

Cath smiled sweetly, though it took effort. "You can try. But I think you'll find I'm not the easily impressed young girl you married."

She didn't want him to try. She wanted him to make things easy for her for once. But he looked as if it would take a tank to budge him, so she gave up. She would remain strong. He'd give up soon, she'd bet on it.

"I'll get the dust cloths and vacuum," she said, turning to escape. There was enough work to keep them both too busy all day long to talk or think. He'd get tired of housework and yearn for the excitement of a natural catastrophe or some war skirmish.

Hell of a way to spend his homecoming, Jake thought as Cath left to get the cleaning supplies. He pushed the curtains wider apart, and was showered in dust. He thought about the fantasies he'd daydreamed on the flight across the Atlantic, him and Cath in bed, only getting up for food from time to time. It didn't look good for that scenario coming true anytime soon. He'd have to convince her what they had was worth saving. Even if it meant making changes on his end. God, he didn't know what he'd do if she really went through with a divorce. He'd been crazy about her from the first day they met.

He loved his job, but he loved his wife more. Didn't she know he'd love to come home every night to be with her? But unless she lived in the troubled spots of the world, that wasn't going to happen.

How many nights had he lain awake in bed, wishing she was there with him, just to hold, to talk to, to kiss? How many days had he taken a break from the grueling schedule and wished she'd shared the quiet afternoon, kicked back and doing nothing but being together?

Did she really think she didn't mean everything to him?

Maybe it was selfish on his part, but he wanted her to want him, be there for him. Want to share what they could together. And for him to be enough for her without having to have others to make a family.

Cath returned, lugging a vacuum and two dust clothes.

"I think you need more than a vacuum to clean these curtains," he said, slapping one. The cloud of dust almost enveloped him.

"I guess you're right," she said, frowning. "Can they be washed do you think?"

He looked at the material. There were spots burned by the sun. The hem looked frayed.

"I'd chuck them and get new ones."

"Another thing to do. If you'll take them down, I'll go hunt up some trash bags."

"Let's pile everything in the yard for the time being. We'll see how much accumulates and then decide if we want to make a run to the dump or if the local trash company can come and pick it up," Jake suggested.

"You're saying you think there'll be a lot of trash?"

"Don't you?"

Cath looked around the room and shrugged. "Maybe. We'll know better after I assess each room."

"You're going through every room in this place?"

"Yes."

"Over this one holiday?"

"You have a problem with that?" she asked, giving him a look.

"It's Christmas, Cath, don't you want to celebrate?"

"Sure, I'll take Christmas Day off."

The last several years she'd spent the day with Abby and her family. Wouldn't she want to decorate and all this year?

"You'll need decorations," he said.

"Give me a break, Jake. When did you ever care about decorating for Christmas?"

"The year we shared it in Washington."

He could tell she remembered. She looked away with sadness. He should have come home for that holiday each year. He could have found a way. Regret began to eat at him for the lost op-portunities. All the more reason to make this one special. To find a way to change her mind.

For a moment a touch of panic swept through him.

What if he was unable to change her mind?

"Whatever. If we get through this room today, I'll look for Aunt Sally's decorations. Funny, I never spent a Christmas with her. I only came in the summers. I wonder if she was lonely on Christmas. She didn't come to visit us. What did she do all those holidays?"

"What will you do over the holidays if we're not married?" he asked. Maybe thinking like a single person would give her a better picture of what life would be. He hoped she hated it.

"Visit with Abby like the last four, I guess," she replied. "Until I meet someone else to marry. Then we'll establish our own Christmas traditions."

He frowned and yanked on the curtains. They ripped at the top and came tumbling down. The dust made him cough. Served him right for letting his temper take control. He was usually cool under trying circumstances. The thought of Cath with someone else, however, made him see red. She was *his wife*. She loved him, he knew she did. He just had to get her to see that she wouldn't be happy with anyone else. He wasn't giving up on their marriage!

She began opening drawers in the dresser as he bundled the curtains up. Heading for the door, he hoped being outside for a few minutes would cool his temper and give him some insight in how to get Cath off the idea of divorce and back into his arms.

Two hours later they were almost finished. Jake was working on the windows, the outside could stand cleaning as well, but he'd need a ladder for that. The room sparkled. The dresser had held little. The closet was empty. The room had obviously been a little-used guest room.

He glanced at Cath, remembering the slinky

nightie he'd picked up in Paris. He had planned to give it to her on Christmas Day, and then have her model it for him. That dream popped like a bubble. She was wearing sweats, on her hands and knees, washing down the dirty floor molding. Her blond hair was pulled back in a ponytail to keep it out of her eyes as she worked. There was nothing romantic or sexy about it, but just looking at her sparked a flare of desire. The thought that she no longer cared enough about him to fight for their marriage hurt. He had to find a way to ignite the flame that once blazed between them.

CHAPTER THREE

JAKE was driving her crazy, Cath thought as she surveyed the clean bedroom, glad to see how nice it looked. Even with the windows bare, it looked much better than when they'd started. Jake had worked as hard as she had. Which was causing problems. She'd believed by now he'd give up and wander away to do something else. But he'd surprised her. He hadn't complained once. Hadn't tried to get out of anything, from carrying the dirty curtains outside, to washing each tiny pane of glass in the tall windows.

Every so often she'd feel his gaze on her. It took all her self-control to keep from looking back. She swallowed hard. She didn't want that tingling awareness when he was near. She certainly didn't need the memories of them together in happier times crowding her mind, of the love that had flowed, the laughter shared. How long ago that seemed.

This was now. Nothing had changed with his arrival, except to throw her into confusion. She dare not believe in happy endings again. She would only be disappointed.

"That's that," he said. "Anything else left here?"

She looked around, loath to leave the task. What would they talk about without the room's work between them? She was too tired to start another room today, yet dreaded having to make conversation. Why couldn't he just leave?

"It looks nice," she said. "Thank you for helping."

"It's what husbands do," he said.

"Stop it, Jake. That's not going to change my mind. You're here for how long before being gone another six months? If you really wanted to change things, you'd start with your job."

"Or you could quit your job and come with me," he said.

She looked at him in disbelief. "I have no desire to go to war zones or spend my life traveling around after you. I did that twice. You were rarely there, and I was far from home and friends. I want a home to be a refuge each night to return to. I like the furnishings and the artwork I chose. I'm not a nomad and have no intentions of becoming one."

"I'm not a nomad. I have a home."

"No, Jake, you have a place to stay when you're in Washington." Cath gathered up the dirty dust rags and reached for the vacuum. She'd put it in the next room for tomorrow's work. Then she wanted to take a quick shower and get rid of the sixteen layers of dust that she'd accumulated during the cleaning.

Looking at Jake, she was surprised to find his expression thoughtful. She'd thought he'd come back with an instant reply, but for once he seemed to be thinking about what she said. And if he followed it through, he'd know she was right.

"I'm going to take a quick shower and then make something for dinner," she said.

"Early for dinner."

"We didn't have lunch and I'm starving."

"Go take a shower. I'll clean up after you're finished," Jake said. "Unless you wish to share the shower?"

The devilish gleam in his eyes caused Cath's heart rate to kick into high. She was not going to give into temptation. She couldn't foresee a future where as former lovers they got together from time to time for old times' sake. The break had to be clean and sharp. And final.

"I'll hurry and try not to use all the water," she said and turned and fled.

Cath put together sandwiches and heated some soup for dinner. It wasn't fancy, but was plenty for the two of them, and would have to do. She wasn't trying to impress anyone with her culinary skills. She was used to making do with abbreviated meals because she didn't feel like cooking at the end of the day when it was for herself alone.

They ate at the kitchen table. Cath was careful to set their places as far apart as practical. Jake said little, digging into the food like a starving man. She realized that except for the coffee he'd made that morning, he'd had nothing to eat all day. She felt guilty and tried to squelch the feeling. Let him fend for himself. But saying it to herself didn't work. She should have offered him something earlier.

"We can look for the Christmas decorations when we finish," he said a few moments later.

"You're serious about decorating?"

"Don't you want to?" he asked.

Cath thought about it for a minute. The house would seem more welcoming if decked out for the holiday. "I guess. I don't know what Aunt Sally might have. And I didn't bring any of our ornaments."

"Is there an attic?"

"Just a small one. My guess is the decorations

would be stored in the cellar with everything else from the last two hundred years."

"That's some cellar."

"I remember going down there when I was a kid and being scared silly. There are cubicles and narrow passageways making it like a maze. Furniture and boxes and old trunks are every where, and cobwebs. Aunt Sally once said the family never threw anything away. I believe her. I guess if she had decorations that's where they'd be, but exactly where is anyone's guess."

"So we go exploring."

Cath wasn't thrilled with the idea, but her curiosity was roused. Aunt Sally must have decorated at the holidays, yet Cath would never know the significance of any of the ornaments. She wondered if her aunt's collection contained any very old baubles or if any had had special meaning to her. She regretted not spending any Christmases with the elderly woman. She should have insisted Aunt Sally spend the last several Christmases with her. Each time she'd invited her, Aunt Sally had given an excuse. Hadn't she been lonely spending the holiday alone?

The dim bulb over the bottom of the cellar steps did not provide much illumination when they started downstairs sometime later. Cath had propped the door open and let Jake lead the way. When they reached the cement floor, he looked around.

"We should have brought a flashlight," he said.

"There's lighting throughout, just not very bright. I don't know if the wiring can stand it, but I'd like to replace every bulb with a brighter one." She found the old light switch and flipped it up. Throughout the cellar lights went on, throwing deep shadows among the items stored there.

"Spooky," she said with a shiver.

He laughed, and reached out to take her hand. "I'll protect you from the bogeyman."

She snatched her hand back. "I can take care of myself." As if to prove that, she stepped to the right and started down one aisle. There were boxes and boxes stacked shoulder high. None were labeled. If they had to look through each one, they could be here all week.

The thought of clearing the cellar was mind-boggling. Cath studied the items as she walked along. There was no way she could clear this area during the holiday break. It would take days to go through things. The furniture alone would be enough to furnish another house. She wandered down one aisle and over to another. The light cast odd shadows. She ran her fingertips over some of the tables, coming away dusty. There were old chests and armoires, chairs and tables. A cradle. She stopped at that and rocked it gently, imagining a baby of her own nestled snugly asleep beside her own bed. The cradle looked old, with hand carvings on the headboard and footboard. The wood was burnished from years of use.

She moved on, opening a drawer here and there, lifting the lids of some of the boxes—clothing from an earlier era, books long forgotten, mementos from ancestors long gone.

She lifted one lid of a very old trunk and saw lace and silk. To one side a small leather-bound book. She took it out and opened it. It looked like a journal of some kind.

"I found them," Jake's voice sounded from a distance.

"I'll be right there." She tucked the book under her arm and closed the trunk. She'd read through it later. Maybe it belonged to one of her ancestors.

"Call again so I can find you," she said.

"I went left from the stairs. You went right, so I'm probably directly across the cellar from you," he said.

She followed the sound of his voice and rounding a corner found him standing in an open area, two boxes of Christmas decorations opened at his feet.

"There're more," he said, pointing to the stack at his right.

"Let's take them upstairs and see what we can use." She reached for the closest box and the journal dropped to the floor.

"What's that?" Jake asked, reaching for it.

Cath scooped it up. "A book I found. It looks like a journal or something and I thought I'd read it."

His hand dropped. "Family history?"

"Maybe." She put it on top of the box, and lifted both. "I'll take these upstairs."

Jake stacked another two boxes on top of each other and followed.

Two more trips and all the boxes of decorations had been brought up to the dining room and put on the large table. Cath placed the journal away from the boxes, for some reason not wanting to share with Jake. Time they broke ties, not made them.

"We need a tree," he said, pulling out a string of lights. "Your aunt must have had a tree each year, and a large one to boot if the number of strings of lights is any indication."

"We don't need a tree."

"Sure we do. I know just the spot in the living room where it should go, in front of the two windows on the front wall," he said.

Cath knew where he meant. Shifting the furniture would center the tree as the focal point of the room.

It would be festive, and more like Christmas, with decorations and a tree. She loved Christmas. But to share it with Jake felt awkward. She wouldn't have bothered on her own. Why should she just because he came home unexpectedly?

"Maybe I'll see about getting one tomorrow," she said reluctantly.

"We'll go together. Let's cut one at a tree farm," he suggested.

Cath looked at Jake with surprise. The one Christmas they'd spent together, they'd picked up a tree at the Boy Scout lot. As she recalled, she'd done most of the decorating, he'd been on the phone with the news bureau.

"I don't know if they have any tree farms around," she said. Nor did she want to get the tree with Jake. It was bad enough having him here, but she didn't want to do things that would build memories. Even if he didn't agree at this moment, he would soon have to acknowledge their separating was the best thing.

"I'll check." He headed to the kitchen and the phone book beneath the telephone.

"Where's Windsor Drive?" he called.

"I have no idea."

"The exchange is the same as this one, so it can't be too far away. We'll call in the morning and find out," Jake said, returning to the dining room, phone book in hand.

"It says it's open seasonally, which has to mean now. And they open at ten. Shall we go there before tackling the next bedroom?" he asked.

Cath felt a shiver of awareness go through her at his tone. She wanted to turn and run away from the powerful attraction the man held for her. If she gave in, he'd only leave in a few days. Leave her with more regrets.

Could they have done things differently at some stage of their marriage?

She looked back at the decorations, many

wrapped in tissue to protect them. A premonition shook her. She should not be going on any
Christmas tree search with Jake. Either she
wanted to end the marriage or not, and doing
things together wasn't ending their relationship.

"I don't think so," she said.

"Why not?" he asked, closing the telephone
book and putting it on the table.

He crossed to her and turned her slowly to
face him. "It's only getting a tree, Cath, what
can that hurt? It's not like it's going to change
anything, is it?"

It would, but how to explain? He made it seem
so innocuous, but she knew it could hold danger.
To her recent decision. She remembered so
many of the happy times together. There had not
been enough of them. But in the end, Jake
always left. And her heart broke a little with
each departure. She needed to make this break
clean, not linger, have second thoughts, or —

"Cath?"

She looked up, into once dear, familiar dark

eyes. Eyes that seemed to see right down to the heart of her. Slowly Jake came closer. He leaned over her until his mouth touched hers, his lips warm and firm, pressing against hers.

For a heartbeat she was where she always longed to be. Then she remembered and pushed against him.

"No, Jake. Leave me alone." She broke away and stepped across the room.

"I don't want you staying here, you know that. But I can't force you to leave. I can insist on your keeping your distance from me, however. If you won't, then I will leave."

"And go where?"

"To Abby's. She invited me for Christmas, I'm sure she would be happy to have me visit."

And not Jake. The unspoken message was clear.

He held up his hands in surrender. "Fine. I'll keep my distance. You keep yours."

"What?" She blinked. She had done nothing.

"Just in case you get a case of the hots for me you can't control," he said audaciously.

Cath wished she were closer, she'd slug him one. He could be so annoying on occasion.

"I'm sure I can control myself," she said primly. Reaching for the diary, she turned and headed for her room. At least she could be alone there. She had a feeling delving into the past would be safer than dealing with the present.

"Wait," he called.

She paused, looking at him over her shoulder.

"What about tomorrow?"

"Get the tree yourself," she said.

She shut the door to her bedroom and went to climb into the bed. It was too early to go to sleep, but she could begin reading the old book. She was tired enough to relish lying down while she did it. Bending and reaching while cleaning had strained muscles beyond their normal use.

Cath covered herself with the top quilt, trying to ignore the fact Jake was downstairs going through Christmas decorations. This wasn't a real Christmas for them, just the last one they'd share together. How sad. Maybe she should spend it with him. He was alone, so was she.

But that would give him false hope. And she was firm in her decision to wrest back her life and put it on a different path.

She lifted the journal, snuggled down beneath the covers and opened the cover. The first words sent a chill through her.

Four days until Christmas. The handwriting was tiny, but legible. Who had written it? Cath looked at the inside cover, but there was no name, no indication what year it was written. The person who wrote it knew who he or she was. The book probably had never been intended for anyone else to see.

Cath couldn't believe she was reading it four days before Christmas. How spooky was that?

I hate this war. At last I heard Jonathan is in North Carolina. Can he return home for Christmas? I pray so. He was at the battle at Kings Mountain, clear across the state. A great distance in the snow. I haven't heard from him since. I wish he'd send word. Or come home. Maybe he is on his way even as I write. I'd give anything for him to stride into our kitchen and say, come here Tansy darlin' and give your husband a kiss.

Was she talking about the Civil War? Cath tried to remember the battles of that war, but Gettysburg kept popping into mind. She'd have to look up Kings Mountain. She wished her memory of history was better.

Mrs. Talaiferro had her boy Ben bring me some butter this morning. He repaired that loose hinge on the hen house for me. I send back some of the ham slaughtered from the hog a few weeks ago. Without neighbors help-ing out, I don't see how I could manage. Farm-ing is really a man's job. Jonathan is so good at it. I hope he's home for the spring planting.
 The nights are lonely. The days are so

short and cold. I can scarcely go outside to gather eggs. My fingers were half frozen by the time I fed the hens and hogs. I hope Jonathan is warm. I sent him a new muffler I knitted, but haven't heard from him in so long, I don't know if he got it or not.

I miss my husband. Please God, let this war end soon. Let the British be driven to the sea!

The British! Cath sat up at that. Was this diary from the time of the Revolutionary War? Who were Tansy and Jonathan? Early relatives of hers? They must be if her journal was in the cellar. As Aunt Sally had always said no one in the family seemed to throw anything away.

Eagerly Cath read more. The pages that followed related the loneliness Tansy felt with her husband absent. Cath wondered how old the writer had been, how long they'd been married. Why was there no other family mentioned? It appeared that Tansy lived alone. Would later pages reveal more? This was obviously not the first journal the woman had kept. Could she find the others? Coming to the end of the entry several pages later, Cath noted the next one started: *Three days until Christmas.*

Closing the book, Cath decided to read each day's entry as it matched her own countdown until Christmas. How odd to find the journal today—on the exact same day it was written. How could she find out about the Battle of Kings Mountain? That would give her an idea of what Christmas Tansy was writing about. Did Jonathan make it home in time for the holiday? She wanted to skip ahead, but refrained. It was tantalizing to have to wait until tomorrow to find out what happened next. But gave her something to look forward to.

She quickly got ready for bed and climbed back in. Drifting off to sleep a short time later, Cath was anxious to return to the cellar for the first time. She'd love to find out more about Tansy. To see if there were more journals, or a portrait or something. She bet her Aunt Sally could have told her about Tansy. If only she'd known about her earlier.

It was pitch-dark when Cath awoke. A nightmare frightened her awake. She lay in bed searching the blackness, feeling the tendrils of the horror reluctantly let her go.

She rolled to her side, eyes wide, straining to see something. The images of men on the battlefield wouldn't go completely away. Blown apart by guns and cannons, everyone had Jake's face.

She shuddered and pushed back the covers. She wanted to shake the fear that coursed through her at the nightmare. Jake was fine, sleeping down the hall. The old diary had sparked the dream—she knew that from the images of the men that had populated it— dressed as farmers and soldiers had so long ago. It was just a bad dream.

She pulled on a thick robe, found her slippers and headed for the kitchen. Some light, warm milk and semblance of normalcy were what she needed. Turning on the hall light, she descended the stairs and padded softly into the kitchen.

Flipping on that light, she was startled to discover Jake, sitting near the window, gazing out at the darkness. Beside him on the table was a bottle of scotch whiskey and a half empty glass.

He turned and looked at her, squinting slightly in the light.

"What are you doing up?" Cath asked. Glancing at the bottle, she raised her eyebrows in surprise. "Where did you get that?"

"Your aunt Sally had a stash." He raised the glass. "To Aunt Sally." Taking a hefty swallow, he carefully placed the glass beside the bottle.

"What time is it?" she asked, glancing at the kitchen clock. It was almost three o'clock in the morning!

"Why aren't you in bed?" she asked.

"Couldn't sleep. This homecoming isn't

exactly what I was looking forward to, you know? Hell of a way to spend Christmas, get slapped in the face with a divorce demand." He turned away.

Cath stared at him. He stared out the window. What could he see in the dark?

"What are you doing up?" he asked a minute later.

"I had a nightmare. I thought some warm milk would help me go back to sleep. Want some?"

He laughed, but the sound held no humor. "No, this'll do me," he said, reaching for the glass again.

"I never knew you to be much of a drinker," Cath said, moving to the refrigerator to get the milk.

"Never had a need before. Trying to forget my sorrows," he mocked.

"Come on, Jake, don't be dramatic."

He slammed his hand down on the table and rose, turning to glare at her.

"Dramatic? Hell of a homecoming, Cath, to an

empty condo and a cold note on the mantel. I drive like a maniac to get here and for what? An icy reception. This is not how I wanted to spend Christmas. I busted my butt getting here. You're talking about leaving me, giving me no chance to change things and blabbering on about finding another man when you're my wife! What do you expect me to do, just sit back and say have at it? Dammit, I'm not going to do that! You won't even go shopping for a blasted Christmas tree with me. What—do I have the plague or something? Cath, I love you. I married you because of that and nothing has changed!"

Cath stared at him, taken aback at his vehemence. She'd never seen Jake so angry, not even when talking about injustice in the world, which really riled him.

She looked at the whiskey bottle. Was that loosening his tongue? She'd wanted to understand how he felt about things. Maybe liquor was the way to go.

He followed her glance and picked up the

bottle, holding it out for a moment, then took a healthy swig from it. "It's the only warm thing in the house right now," he said, setting the bottle back on the table.

Taken aback, Cath opened her mouth to defend herself. Then thought better of it. She tried to see things from his point of view. She'd been thinking of this separation all fall, had discussed it endlessly with Abby. But she'd only given him a vague clue in all her e-mails. Essentially he'd walked into the situation cold.

He'd expected Christmas at home, and she'd been gone.

Had he been as lonely as she during the months apart? Did he sometimes wish things would be different?

Guilt played on her. She should have told him in her letters which way she was thinking. Should have given him a chance to open a discussion before now. Cath tried to be fair, and if she were fair to Jake, she would ease up some. They were only together for another few days. She could be cordial during that time. They'd married thinking they'd be together forever. She'd known when she married him what his job was. Just because she couldn't cope wasn't a reason to condemn the man. The fault lay with her.

"Okay, I'll go get the tree with you," she said before she thought.

He looked at her, then at the bottle. "Gee, thanks a bunch for the mighty concession." He picked up the bottle and walked out of the room.

Cath stared at the place he'd stood, hearing the echo of his anger. Tears filled her eyes. She never thought he'd care. She thought she'd be the only one to mourn the ending of their marriage. But maybe she'd been wrong about Jake.

Turning to the stove, she blinked, trying to clear her vision. Once the milk heated, she added cinnamon and poured it into a mug. She left the pan soaking in the sink. Carefully carrying the mug of warmed milk, she turned off the lights behind her. She didn't hear anything from Jake's room. Her heart ached that he'd drink himself stupid because of her. It was so unlike the man. Or at least the man she thought she knew.

Going into her bedroom, she wondered what else she could have done. Written him sooner? But if he thought the letter on the mantel was cold, what would he have thought of an e-mail telling him they were through?

She could have discussed it with him—if he'd ever come home. Even today, when he'd tried to talk about it, she'd been stubbornly reticent—saying only she wanted it to end.

She slipped into bed and sipped her milk. She was feeling as melancholy as Tansy had sounded in her diary. She could relate to the loneliness Tansy wrote about. How many nights had she lain in bed wishing so hard that Jake was with her? How many days had she gone through the motions of living, always feeling a part of her was missing? Did Jonathan come back to Tansy? Did they have a long and happy life together?

They were probably her great-great-great or more grandparents. She should find out about them before the end of the holiday.

As to what to do with the house, Cath was growing attached to it. She liked the location on the banks of the wide James River. She was in the country, yet only a short distance from Williamsburg, and not too far from the bigger cities of Norfolk and Richmond. It was a lovely, ideal setting in which to raise children.

A pang struck her. She'd so love to have a child with Jake, a little boy with his daddy's dark hair and eyes, or a small girl with Jake's determination and observation traits. But she didn't want to raise a child alone. She wanted its father actively involved. Home for school events, and soccer meets, to have the house filled with love and laughter. But it wasn't going to happen and she had to let go those dreams and forge new ones.

She'd find a man to love. A man who wanted what she wanted, a home, a close-knit family that shared every aspect of living. And together they'd have a perfect future.

She just had to get through this holiday with Jake.

CHAPTER FOUR

THE next morning was blustery. The wind blew the bare trees, snapping them back and forth at its whim. The sky was a steel-gray, clouds roiling along the path of the wind.

Cath gazed out the kitchen window. There were whitecaps on the river. It looked cold and miserable. She didn't want to go out at all, much less to search for a tree. She set the coffee to brew and pulled down a box of her favorite cereal. She wasn't cooking breakfast this morning.

She filled her bowl and got the milk. A movement outside caught her eye and she leaned over the sink to see better. Jake was walking along the bank of the river, hands in his pockets, head bent against the wind. He stopped opposite the window and gazed out across the river for a long moment. She wondered what he was doing out there. Then she wondered if he were freezing. His jacket didn't seem heavy enough for the wind that was gusting.

For a long moment Cath watched Jake. He seemed frozen in place. What was he thinking? Any regrets about their marriage? Or was he miles away at some newsworthy site, wondering how long before he'd be back in the field again?

When he turned and began walking toward the house, she darted away from the window. Pouring the milk on her cereal, she sat down just as he came in the back door. It would weaken her stance if he knew how much she longed to be with him. If he'd only agree to stay home, they could make the best future in the world. But that would mean changing almost everything about him, and Cath didn't see that happening.

"Morning," he said, closing the door behind him. It slammed when the wind snapped it from his hand.

"Good morning," Cath replied. "Coffee's ready and there's cereal for breakfast. What were you doing outside so early?" Especially after your late night, she wanted to add, but prudently didn't voice the thought.

"I wanted to see some of the river. Could you have a dock here? Maybe a small boat to take out on the water?"

"I guess. I never asked Aunt Sally. She was in her sixties when I first started coming during the summers. She had a neighbor a few doors down who had a boat, which they tied to a small dock. I used to go out in it a lot. We'd even swim from the dock in the hot weather. The river current isn't that strong."

"Nice house and yard. You have a lot of land around it."

"An acre, I think it is."

He poured himself a cup of coffee. Cath watched him as she ate. He didn't seem any the worse for wear after last night.

She was still a bit shaken from her nightmare,

and from the poignant words from Tansy. Which reminded her.

"What do you know about a battle at Kings Mountain?" she asked.

"We won it," he said, getting a bowl and spoon. He snagged the box of cereal and filled his bowl. Sitting near Cath, he reached for the milk.

"When was it?"

He looked at her in puzzlement. "It was during the Revolutionary War. One of the battles that began changing the tide for the colonists. Can't remember exactly when it was, but I think it wasn't too long afterward that Washington met Cornwallis at Yorktown, maybe a year or so. So maybe 1780, around there."

"Imagine that," Cath said softly, amazed she had a journal from the 1700s.

"Why do you want to know about Kings Mountain?" he asked.

"It's mentioned in that diary I found yesterday. I want to see if I can find others. I didn't realize it was so old. The leather is still in good condition, the writing a bit faded, but it's not deteriorating like I'd think a book that old would."

"Probably not made like paper was later. If it's from the 1700s rags were the primary component, lasted much longer than the later wood pulp paper. Are you still going with me to get that tree?"

"I don't know. It looks cold outside." She was having second thoughts, and thirds. Being with him and not hoping for a future was almost more than she could bear. She wanted him to storm in and say he loved her more than anything—even his job—and would never leave.

"It's cold and blustery and threatening to storm. We might have snow before night. But it feels good after the heat of the Middle East. Bundle up, you won't freeze," he said.

So much for a promise never to leave.

They ate in silence. Cath was afraid to disturb the quiet. She hadn't a clue what Jake was thinking. At the end of the holiday, would he quietly go back to work and let her get the divorce uncontested? Or would he argue against it for whatever reason, and then take off? The only thing she knew for certain, he would not be remaining long in Washington.

Glancing at the kitchen clock, she saw it was too early to go for the tree, yet she didn't want to get started on another room until after they got back. She knew how dirty she'd get.

"I sorted through some of the decorations last night," Jake said, rising to take his bowl to the sink. "I even tested the lights. Most work. We can get replacements at a store. You'll like the ornaments...your aunt had some unusual ones."

Cath looked out the window at the signs of the wind. She wasn't sure she wanted to go tree hunting in the best of times, and today's weather didn't qualify for best. Why had she agreed to go?

Promptly at ten they arrived at the tree farm. Despite it being so close to Christmas, they were not the only ones there, but the other two families had a half dozen children between them running around, exclaiming which tree was the biggest and begging their parents to buy it quick before someone else got it.

"Cut it yourself or we'll do it," the man by the gate said. He gestured to saws and small hatchets.

Jake looked at them and then at Cath.

"At the risk of proving totally inept, I say we try cutting it ourselves," he said.

"Don't look at me, I know nothing about being a lumberjack."

The man on the stool laughed. "Nothing to it, ma'am. Just cut near the ground, level so it'll set right in your stand. No need to be a lumberjack."

Jake laughed and took a small saw. He started down one row.

Cath followed slowly, watching the children. If they had had children earlier, their kids would be running around now, excited about getting a tree. What an exciting time holidays were with children. The boys and girls were having such fun running up and down the rows. She could just imagine that fun continuing after they chose their tree. They'd go home and each mother and father would encourage them to decorate it. Ornaments that were family heirlooms would be lovingly placed on the branches. Maybe each child would get a special ornament commemorating this Christmas. Tinsel would be hung—carefully by the mother, and thrown on by children. Laughter, hot chocolate, dreams would be shared. She wanted those happy days for herself. She wanted a family.

Jake was way ahead of her when she looked for him. She hurried down the aisle, thinking how bland the outing was with just the two of them.

When she caught up with him, she was startled by the happiness in his eyes.

"I measured the space in the living room and we can have a seven foot tree. This starts the seven footers," he said, pointing to a tree a few inches taller than he was.

Cath hadn't even thought about that aspect.

"Did you see those kids?" she asked, looking back down where they were.

"Yeah, noisy, weren't they?"

"Jake! They're so excited about getting a tree. I can't wait until I have children to share days like this with them."

He looked away. When she glanced at him, the happiness had faded. Was that sadness she saw in his gaze? A reminder that if she had children, it would be with another man. She'd start a family without Jake.

The thought pierced like a knife. She couldn't imagine another man filling her heart like Jake had. Would there be anyone else for her? Or was she risking a long and lonely future by saying goodbye?

He didn't like the idea of her with someone else, yet he refused to do anything about them. He had his job, she wished him joy in it. Surely he could see there was no future for the two of them.

"This is a nice tree," she said, trying to get the expedition over with. It was safer back at the house. She wasn't trying to make things any more difficult than they were. But if he thought taking her to buy a tree would repair six years of neglect, he had to have rocks in his head.

"If that's the one you like, I'll cut it down."

She could be imagining the disappointment in his tone, but she wasn't sure. It wouldn't hurt to extend the expedition a little longer. "Oh, wait. Let's look at a couple more. Just to be sure."

They spent more than a few minutes looking at different trees. While the conifers had been trimmed to conform to a perfect shape, there were slight imperfections in each one.

Jake commented on some, Cath on others until they had been there almost an hour, and not settled on a tree.

"I'm freezing," she said. The earlier families had left. Another group had shown up. The tree farm seemed to be doing a good business for three days prior to Christmas.

"I wanted that last tree. Agree with me so we can cut it down and head for home," she said. "My fingers may have frostbite."

"It's not that cold. If that's the one you want, I'll settle for it."

"Settle? It's a gorgeous tree!"

"It has a gap near the bottom."

"Put that side next to the wall. I want that tree!"

"Fine, we'll take that one. We also need to stop at the store on the way home, to get the bulbs for the burned out lights. Do we need tinsel?" he reminded her.

Cath walked around her chosen tree slowly, examining it from top to bottom. There was one bare spot, but not a large one, it could be right next to the wall where no one would see it. The fragrance filled the air. It would be wonderful in Aunt Sally's old house.

Not that anyone would see the tree except Jake and her. They had no friends here, had not invited anyone to share the day with them. Still, she wanted it to look nice—in honor of using

Aunt Sally's ornaments, she told herself. But mostly she wanted to get out of the cold.

"Glad that's settled," she said in mock frustration. She laughed, feeling joy rising at the thought of decorating it. Christmas had always been her favorite holiday. "Can you cut it?" she asked.

"I can try. Hold it steady as I cut through the trunk."

Jake knelt down and applied the saw. When the tree began to wobble, Cath grabbed hold and held on, trying to keep it upright. With a final swipe of the saw, the tree tumbled onto her, engulfing her completely in fragrant branches.

"Ohhh, get it off me before we both fall," Cath called, giggling at the unexpected fun.

Jake pulled it away, and gently tipped it into the pathway. "Grab the top, I'll get the trunk and we'll carry it to the car."

"Will it fit on the car? It's huge!"

"We'll tie it on top. Hope it won't cover the windshield."

With the help of the lot owner, they tied the

tree on the car. After paying him, Jake opened the passenger door for Cath.

"Next stop that store we passed when we turned on Winston, then home," he said.

"I'll stay in the car to make sure no one steals our tree. It's a pretty one, isn't it?" she asked.

"Lovely," he said, but his eyes weren't on the tree, they were on her.

Cath caught her breath, almost swept away by the light in Jake's eyes.

She looked ahead, motioning him to close the door. "I'm cold, shut the door." She was not getting caught up in some romantic notion that getting a tree together changed anything. It was another memory to cherish. But it also signified the end of a relationship. Her heart ached with the thought of no more Christmases with Jake.

As he rounded the car, she saw another family walking to their car, all four children struggling to hold on to the large tree. The mother and father exchanged loving smiles.

Cath caught her breath and looked away. She

needed to hold on to her dream, and ignore the temptation that called to her. She wanted her own family, not a man who spent most of his life half way round the world!

It was early afternoon by the time they turned into the road that Aunt Sally's house was on. Jake was satisfied their outing had been a step in the right direction. Cath had been distant at the beginning, but warmed up to the fun of finding a tree as the morning went on. She'd been laughing at the end. He knew she'd mentioned clearing and cleaning another bedroom this afternoon, but he had a feeling she'd rather decorate their tree.

He'd bought some cider in the store and some Christmas cookies. They weren't homemade, but would do in a pinch.

As they pulled into the long driveway the cell phone in Cath's purse rang.

"Expecting someone?" he asked.

"No," she said, rummaging around in the purse and pulled out her phone.

"Hello?" Cath listened a moment, then gave him an odd look.

"I know, Abby. He's here now."

So her friend was calling to warn her. Interesting.

"The phone was in my purse which I left on the kitchen counter. Unless I was in that room when you called, I wouldn't have heard it ring."

She was silent another moment.

"It's okay," she said slowly.

Jake would bet Abby asked how things were going between them. Jake squelched the urge to reach for the phone and tell Abby to mind her own business. He and Cath would work things out. But Cath was acting more emotional than usual and he had to walk warily around her. Alienating her by being rude wouldn't help.

Jake slowly got out of the car. He could stay and listen to one half of the conversation, or get going on unloading the tree and enticing Cath to forget cleaning the old house and concentrate on decorating it instead.

Though if she insisted on cleaning this afternoon, he'd suggest the room he was using. She had done nothing to make him feel welcomed. His room wasn't dusted or aired. He'd just collapsed on the bed both last night and the first night and made do with the covers that were there. He'd slept in worse, so hadn't complained, but a bit of the welcome he had hoped to find upon returning home would have helped.

"Want to help me take the tree inside?" he asked, peering back into the car.

Cath turned, frowning when she saw him. "Oh. Sure. I'm going to have to go, Abby. I'll call you later." He could almost feel the dismay when she realized he was still there. Tough.

Angrily he turned and began to untie the tree. Cath had enjoyed the morning. He knew she had. Now the phone call brought back her intent with a vengeance. Time was fleeting. It was already three days until Christmas. If he didn't make some progress soon, she'd be returning to

Washington before he knew it and to the divorce she wanted so passionately.

He had to find a way to turn that passion toward their marriage.

Dragging the tree off the car, he waited for her to get the light end and they carried it to the front of the house.

"Lean it against the railing. I'll get something to make a stand," he said.

"Try the carriage house. Aunt Sally had tools and other things there. Maybe some scrap wood," she said. "I'll get the things from the car." Gone was the excitement she'd displayed when finding the tree. Now it was back to the business of ending a marriage.

Jake headed for the carriage house in the rear, wishing Abby hadn't called. A man could only stand so much. He needed time to get his emotions under control. It wouldn't pay to make himself look like a fool by railing at Cath. He had time and a hope from the response she'd given when he kissed her. She wasn't immune to him, or out of love, despite what she was saying. She couldn't be.

The carriage house hadn't been used for horses in decades. It had served as Aunt Sally's garage and catch-all—what the cellar didn't hold looked like it was out here. There was a workbench of sorts along one wall. In the back was an old carriage, rotten wheels and all. The cleared space on the right had held Sally's car until she'd given up driving several years prior to her death.

Jake rummaged around the area and found some loose wooden boards. Taking the hammer and some nails from the workbench, he banged together a makeshift stand and headed back to the tree.

His optimism restored, Jake set to work. He liked challenges. He had to get through to Cath. One way or another, he would do it or die trying.

Cath was feeling oddly flustered. She hadn't expected to enjoy getting the tree, but the outing had ended up being fun. And she loved the tree they'd selected. Her arms were full of the packages from the store, more lights, tinsel and a star for the top. The tree itself was thick and full, and smelled so divine it would keep the house fragrant for days.

They could use Aunt Sally's decorations and make it beautiful. But for a moment, she wanted to flee to a dirty bedroom and plunge into cleaning. It was safer than making Christmas memories with Jake.

She looked at the old house. How many Christmases had it known? Had Aunt Sally decorated it each year, or being alone, had only the minimum ornaments displayed to mark the occasion?

She couldn't believe she never inquired after her aunt's practices. She'd invited her to spend the holidays with them more than once, but Aunt Sally had always said she liked to be in her own home at Christmas.

For a moment, Cath wondered if she should

decorate. She loved classroom decorations with all the children participating, chaotic, frenzied though it was. She looked forward to it every year. And to helping Abby decorate her home with her two children. Cath loved decorating their condo, too, though it was only seen by herself and a few friends. Always, every year, she hoped Jake would make it home for the holiday. If she moved here, she'd want all the trappings of family and home. Maybe she should make this year a practice run. Next Christmas she'd know what else to plan on. Maybe outlining the old house in outside lights.

Jake came around the side of the house, boards and hammer in hand.

"Do you know what you're doing?" she asked. She didn't believe she'd ever seen Jake with a hammer in hand.

"I did this as a kid," he said.

She was surprised. Jake rarely talked about his past. His father had died when he'd been nine and his mother had remarried to a man who hadn't liked Jake. She knew he'd been an unhappy teenager who had had to live in a family with new babies and happiness all around—except for him.

"I think this will hold," he said a few moments later. He righted the tree and stepped back. It remained standing, tall and straight.

He looked over at the front door. "Open that and we'll take the tree in that way. I need your help to keep the branches from dragging."

Cath went through the kitchen, dropping her packages, and continued on to the front door. She flung it wide and went to help Jake with the tree.

In only a few moments they had it situated between the two front windows. The fragrance of pine filled the room. Cath thought the place felt warmer just by having the tree. Maybe they could find some logs and have a fire. She'd love an old-fashioned Christmas. Maybe it would even snow as Jake had predicted.

She watched Jake as he turned the tree slightly, hiding the bare spot. What was she going to do with him for the next few days? Surely he'd get bored and head for more exciting places before Christmas. She fully expected him to leave at the first sign of any breaking news.

"I'm going to fix lunch," Cath said. She was torn with the desire to decorate and the need to put distance between herself and Jake.

As she walked down the hall, she heard Jake's cell phone ring. So it happened earlier than she thought.

She took her time making sandwiches. There was nothing she wanted to prepare for dinner. Maybe she'd go out. She could head for Williamsburg, find a place to eat and then wander around the shops that were decorated for the holidays.

Jake came in just as she began to eat. His plate with a sandwich and some chips was at his place.

"Thanks," he said, taking the chair. He ate two bites before looking at her.

"We can put on the lights and ornaments this afternoon."

She shrugged. "I need to get the rooms cleaned, if I want to stay on schedule."

"Hire a service," he said. "It's a holiday, take some time off."

"It's not just the cleaning, I'm trying to assess what to do with everything—the furniture and knickknacks."

He ate in silence for a few minutes.

"Was that your office that called?" she asked, unable to resist.

He nodded.

"A new assignment?"

"No."

If he thought she was going to play twenty questions, he didn't know her. But curiosity burned. Who had called?

"Tell you what," Jake said. "Let's clean Aunt Sally's old room, then after dinner, we'll build a fire in the fireplace and decorate the tree. Tomorrow we'll decorate the rest of the house if you like."

She looked at him suspiciously. How had he known she wanted a fire in the fireplace?

"Maybe."

"For heaven's sake, Cath. Stop blowing hot and cold. Let's agree to spend this Christmas together in harmony. We can make decisions about the future before the New Year, but let's take the next few days for ourselves."

She grudgingly admitted to herself she would have been shocked if Jake had just up and told her out of the clear blue that he wanted to end their marriage. Maybe she needed to give him time to get used to the idea without sniping at each other. It wasn't as if she no longer cared about the man. That was the problem. She was beginning to think she would never get over Jake Morgan.

"I'm not blowing hot and cold. I'll agree to spend the few days until Christmas in harmony. But no talking about the future, one way or the other. And no trying to get me to change my mind," she said, wondering what she'd do if she never did find someone else to love. She'd end up an old lady living in a big house all alone like her great-aunt.

"Fine. Tell me about your work," he said.

"What?"

"You pointed out I don't know a lot about where you work, or your co-workers except for Abby. So tell me."

Cath thought about it for a moment, then nodded and began to tell him about a typical day, mentioning her children—the sweet ones and the troublemakers. She talked about how excited she was each year to be encouraging a new group of students to do their best, to learn what they could and to establish good study habits.

He listened without interruption, watching her as she talked, his eyes narrowed as if assessing all she said.

She didn't care, she loved sharing that part of her life with him. She had all along but he had never seemed interested before. She loved working as a teacher, and was happy she got to see her students for another few years after her class before they went on to other schools.

"What about the other teachers?" he asked at one point. She had refilled their beverage glasses, the sandwiches long gone.

"Except for Abby, I don't interact all that much with the other teachers —not away from school. I do share yard duty with Brent Mulphy and Stella Hawkins. We keep an eye on the students when they take recess. Of course Abby and I have been friends for years."

"No trouble with parents?"

"One or two each term, but nothing I can't handle."

He shook his head. "A room full of eight-year-olds, sounds more intimidating than front line firing to me."

She smiled. "I love children. And that's the best age, in my opinion. They can read, they've started doing more complicated math than just addition and subtraction, and they aren't in their snotty stage of life."

"Ever think of moving into administration?"

She shook her head. "I love teaching. And I'm good at it. That's why I think I could get a job down here without too much trouble."

He pushed his plate away. "You're serious about moving here?"

"I'm seriously thinking about it," she said carefully.

His cell rang again. He fished it out of his jeans pocket, checked the caller and frowned. "I need to take this."

Cath rose and gathered their dishes as Jake headed for the front of the house. She rinsed, dried and put away the plates, and headed upstairs. She wanted to keep to her timetable on clearing the house, but when she stood in Aunt Sally's old bedroom, she paused. Jake's duffel was on the floor, opened, a few items of clothing spilling out. His laptop was closed, sitting on top of the dresser. She never understood how the thing stood up to the casual abuse he gave it. Stuffing it in a duffel, under his arm, or in a backpack didn't seem her idea of ways to handle a sensitive piece of equipment like that. But it seemed to work fine instead of being totally wrecked with his usage.

Looking at the old furnishings in the large room, including the tall secretary with books behind the glass doors, Cath thought about the journal she found. Would there be others in Aunt Sally's bookcase? Or in other boxes in the cellar? She hadn't read but one entry and was anxious to know more about Tansy and Jonathan. Maybe Jake would let her use his laptop to research historical sites so she could see what she could find out about the battle at Kings Mountain.

"Ready to work?" he asked, joining her before she knew it. She had been woolgathering if she missed hearing him climb the stairs.

"This is the largest of the bedrooms. Maybe I should wait and do it last," she said, feeling daunted by the task.

"I wouldn't mind a clean room to sleep in."

Another pang of guilt with the cavalier way she'd treated him. He deserved better.

"You're right. There are clean sheets in the cupboard. They might be a bit musty, but that's all there is. Let's get going."

The afternoon went fast as they developed a working relationship that melded their different abilities. Jake brought down the old curtains and hauled them away. He moved the furniture for Cath to clean behind and beneath, then pushed them back.

Since she'd already donated all of Aunt Sally's clothing last summer, there was little in the room beyond the furnishings. All knickknacks were confined to the large secretary desk, along with several shelves of books.

"You'll need to check to see if any of these are worth anything," he said, opening the double glass doors and reaching for a couple of books, leafing through the volumes.

"The lawyers did an appraisal for inheritance taxes. No first editions or anything," she murmured, scanning the spines of the books. One looked like a journal. She pulled it from the second shelf and opened it. It was, but written by Aunt Sally herself, many years previously. Cath would like to read it, but right now her focus was on finding out more about the lonely woman whose writings she'd found yesterday.

It was dark outside by the time they finished the room. They made the bed, and Cath tried not to think about their large king-size bed at home. It had seemed too large for one person whenever Jake was gone from home. Cath had even thought about using their guest room, but she felt close to him in their bed, so never moved out of the room.

Jake put his duffel on a chair when she mopped the hardwood floor. A good coat of wax would go a long way to making the floor look good. She surveyed the room when finished. Almost all traces of Aunt Sally had disappeared. Jake's things now dominated. She turned, not liking the yearning that seemed to rise every time she looked at Jake.

Cath was tired, and not in the mood to get dressed enough to go out once she showered. Soup and sandwiches again, it looked like. Jake might count himself lucky to be getting out of a marriage if that's all she fed him.

"How about we order pizza?" Jake suggested as he prepared to haul the last of the rags and trash downstairs. "Saves us going out, or either of us cooking. Go take your shower and I'll call in the order. It'll probably be here by the time you're through and I grab a quick shower."

If she let herself think about it, it would seem just like being married. Which of course they were, but they had so little experience in acting like a married couple. They ate out a lot when Jake was home. He claimed he didn't want her to have to spend time in the kitchen when she could be with him. But he sometimes joined her in preparing meals. He had on several occasions, and she almost smiled at the memories. So much of their marriage had been spent apart.

But there was nothing to complain about when they'd been together.

"That sounds good," she said, glad not to even have to heat soup.

Cath quickly showered and changed into comfortable slacks, a warm sweater and house slippers. She passed Jake on the stairs when she headed down. He held out his wallet.

"Pay the guy if he shows up before I get out."

She took it, still warm from his body. The leather was soft and supple. It was stuffed with money, credit cards and his driver's license. She flipped it open. Facing her was an annual school photo teachers got each year. She'd given him this one several years ago. She hadn't known he kept it in his wallet. It made her feel funny. Hadn't he said thinking of her kept him going sometimes? Did he pull out the wallet and look at the photo often?

She felt sad at the thought of him thousands of miles away and as lonely as she was. Where had they gone wrong? Could anything be fixed?

CHAPTER FIVE

As soon as they finished the pizza, Cath pleaded tiredness and escaped to her room. She wasn't as tired as she said, just unable to face an evening with Jake, trying to keep her distance when half the time she yearned to feel his strong arms around her, wanted to hear the steady beat of his heart beneath her ear. She wasn't in the mood to decorate a tree. Being with him was an exercise in trying to ignore her rising awareness. She wished she knew more about what he'd been doing since she'd seen him last. How much danger he'd been in, did he get enough to eat? What did he do for recreation?

But to ask would give rise to his thinking she was mellowing and maybe even reconsidering her decision. She didn't plan to give any false or overly optimistic messages. Her decision had been hard fought, and she couldn't allow emotions to cloud the issue.

She took the journal and pulled the afghan from the bed, going to the chair near the window. It was a bit drafty, but the wool afghan would keep her warm. The light on the small table gave a softness to the room that enabled Cath to imagine how it had looked in the days before electricity, when candles and oil lamps had been the means of illumination.

The entry began:

Three days until Christmas. It began to snow today. I worry about Jonathan getting through the drifts. His horse is old, if still alive. He talked about fighting on foot in the last letter I received from him. If it snows, do they cease fighting? He made no mention of the warm muffler I sent in that hastily scribbled missive. Had he not received it? I sent it with Master

Jerome who was riding to rejoin the regiment. I fear Jonathan will get a chill and pray he doesn't get sick. I wish he would come home for Christmas. He said he would try.

I'm so lonely with him gone. I miss him so. Maybe if I had babes to care for my mind would not dwell on my husband. But our marriage is young and I don't like the days slipping away without him here.

I worry about him. Would that I could go where he goes, keeping some kind of accommodation for him to make sure he eats properly and stays warm and dry. It is probably very shocking of me, but I miss lying in his arms at night. I felt so safe and cherished with him holding me close. It's this horrible war that is making things so difficult. When will it end?

Cath gazed off into space, feeling warm and safe in the room, despite the slight draft. She could empathize with the longing and worry of the long-ago Tansy. Hadn't she lain in bed at night worrying about Jake, wondering if he were all right? How long after he was injured or killed would it have been before she heard anything? Unlike the Revolutionary War days, communications were much faster now. Still, in war zones, or disaster areas, difficulties cropped up making communications impossible. She'd been kept awake long into the night many times, worrying about hearing from him. Imagining him dying far from home, and far from her.

She shivered. He was safe. Maybe he was one of those individuals blessed through danger. He thrived on it. It scared her to death when she learned of some of the situations he'd come through unscathed. How long could his luck hold?

Maybe she should have thoughts like Tansy, going with Jake, to make sure he ate right. He was too thin, she'd noticed that on the first night. And she wasn't doing much to help him gain back that weight. Soup and sandwiches and pizza weren't a substitute for good nutrition.

Feeling restless, Cath laid down the journal and pushed aside the afghan. She rose and went to the stairs. The light was on in the living room. Slowly she descended and walked quietly to the door of the front room.

Jake was winding lights around the tree. The bottom third of the tree had been encircled, he was now working on the upper branches. He had all the lights on, and the sparkling spots of color shimmered in the tears that filled her eyes.

Alone. It seemed so sad to decorate a Christmas tree alone. She had not done it in recent years, preferring to spend the day with her friend Abby and her family. At the condo, she'd have lots of other decorations, but not a tree.

Watching Jake, her heart felt a tug of sadness. He'd come home expecting to celebrate the holidays with her and she'd been gone. According to him, he'd done extraordinary things to get this time and she had shoved it back in his face. He had nowhere else to go, except back to the dangerous places that made news. He and his family had been estranged for years. He'd never returned home after leaving for college.

She blamed his mother for her total switch of allegiance when she remarried. How sad for her son. She would never understand how the woman could ignore her firstborn child. Granted her other children needed her love as well, but to turn from her first was inconceivable to Cath.

Maybe their own marriage wasn't going to last. But she could be kind enough, generous enough to offer him one happy last holiday together.

"Jake?"

He looked over at her. "I thought you went to bed."

"No, I wanted to rest for a little while. I was reading. Why didn't you wait until tomorrow? We could have done this together."

"Really? I got the feeling you didn't want anything to do with me," he said, turning back to the tree. "If I wanted to see it decorated, I had to do it myself."

She stepped into the room.

"I haven't had a tree since the one we got together on our second Christmas," she said slowly. The ornaments they'd brought up from the cellar had been put on the coffee table, the lids of the boxes off so each one could easily be seen. There were globes and spirals, fancy ones and plain. Each held a memory for her great-aunt, lost now to the ages.

"I can help," she said lowly.

He glanced over and shook his head. "Not if it's a chore, Cath. I don't know a lot about holidays, usually working right through them as if they were any other day, but I do know they should be celebrated. Doing it as an obligation doesn't work."

"Christmas used to be my favorite holiday," she said, lifting a shiny ornament and studying it. She remembered the days her parents had made so special for her. Lots of presents, big ham dinner with biscuits, sweet potatoes and of course plum pudding. Her mouth watered for some of that dessert, usually made months before the holidays and brought out as a special treat.

"As I said, usually just another day for me," Jake said.

"What about when you were a child? It had to be special then."

She watched as his expression turned bleak. She wished she hadn't brought it up.

"Maybe when I was young. But it all changed after my dad died."

She knew some of the story, how his mother's new family became more important than her first child. How his stepfather and he had never gotten along, and his mother always sided with the man. Jake had earned a scholarship for college and left home, never to return.

Cath had wished for brothers and sisters as she'd grown up, but when she'd learned of Jake's family life, she'd been glad to be spared that. How awful not to feel loved and cherished as her family made her feel.

As Jake had made her feel in the early days of their marriage.

As he still could.

"What?" he said, catching her gaze.

"I was remembering," she said softly. "We started out so great, why did it go wrong?"

"I don't think anything went wrong," he said.

She snapped out of her mood. "Well it did." She turned and searched the box for a hook for the ornament. "When you get the lights on, I'll start with the ornaments," she said, looking for the box of hooks they'd bought earlier. She'd get the ornaments ready to hang. It would give her something to do, besides being melancholy about Tansy and her Jonathan being separated so long, or her and Jake's situation.

For several awkward moments they continued working. Cath's nerves stretched thin. She moved around the boxes until Jake was behind her and she couldn't see him, hoping it would calm the rampaging awareness that had her as antsy as a cat in a room full of rocking chairs.

She could still hear him moving, hear the soft swish of the branches as he fastened the lights.

"We need Christmas carols," she said at last, almost about to explode. She looked around the room, but saw nothing that looked like a radio or CD player.

"I think there're some records in the room off the dining room," Jake said.

"Records?"

"I take it your aunt was a bit old-fashioned," he said. "Though I wouldn't have expected it."

Jake had met Aunt Sally at their wedding where she and he had hit it off. Cath and Jake had spent a long weekend with Aunt Sally that first year. He hadn't been able to come to visit after that—work.

She left the room, not wanting to think about the past. Or the present. What she should focus on was the future. The glorious future when she'd have lots of family around her at holidays and not feel sad and lonely.

She found the record player and a cabinet full

of albums. Skimming through them quickly, she found several Christmas carol albums bunched together. In less than ten minutes, she had the record player hooked up in the living room and the sound of carols filled the room.

"I thought everyone had CDs now," she commented, resuming her task of putting hooks on ornaments. She had worked through two boxes and was starting on the third.

"What else goes on before the ornaments?" Jake asked, looking at the tree.

"The garland. That silvery thing."

"I know what a garland is," he said, lifting it from one box.

When the record player changed, the song "Silver Bells" began. Jake looked at her, and then stepped over, sweeping her into his arms.

"What are you doing?" she asked, startled.

"Dancing," he said, moving them around the large living room.

Cath laughed. "It's hardly dance music."

"Sure it is, we're dancing, aren't we?" He

danced with an ease that belied his years in rough places. It was as if he did it all the time.

Cath started to protest, the words dying on her lips. This was fun. She loved to dance and had done so little over the length of their marriage. Giving herself up to the moment, she swayed with the music, following Jake's lead, imagining them at a huge Christmas ball. She'd be wearing a sexy red dress—for the season, and for sex appeal. Jake would be in a dark suit, or even a tux. She knew he looked fabulous in a tux; he'd worn one to their wedding.

They'd dance the night away.

When the song ended, the next one was definitely not one to dance to. Slowly they came to a halt.

She looked up into his face, still caught up by the magic of the moment. "Thank you," she said.

"Thank you," he replied, and kissed her.

Still held in his arms, Cath didn't have to move an inch. She let herself continue in the magic, kissing him back, reveling in the sensations so long missing from her life. His body was strong against hers, his muscles a complement to her softer curves. She'd always felt special with Jake—that hadn't changed. The old memories and affection swelled and she let the future fade for a moment. Capturing the present was as good as it got.

Jake ended the kiss slowly. He wanted to carry his wife up the stairs and make love to her all night long. But he hesitated. She'd been as much a participant in the kiss as he had been. Her breathing attested to the fact. He didn't want to spook her. He wasn't going to settle for one night. And if he pushed the issue, he knew she could kick him out and refuse to see him again.

She opened her eyes and looked at him. The temptation to sweep her up was almost more than he could resist. She looked beautiful.

"I bought cider and Christmas cookies today. Want some?" he asked, hoping she wouldn't comment on the fact they shouldn't be kissing if they were getting a divorce. He wasn't sure he could handle that discussion tonight.

"Sure. Want the cider warmed?"

"Of course."

They went into the kitchen, just like old married folks, he thought wryly. Which in a way they were. But this was only their second Christmas together. How had he let work keep him away?

He opened the package of cookies while Cath heated the cider. Sitting at the table, he watched her, wishing so many things had been different. Knowing the future wasn't going to go like he wanted and helpless to change anything. He should be used to it. Life had not gone the way he'd expected since his father died so long ago.

"Tomorrow I have to get back to my schedule," she said.

"Cleaning another room?"

"Yes. One way or another, I want this place ready for whatever I decide by the time I leave at New Year's."

"Are you serious about moving here?" he

asked. Another drawback. He couldn't see living in this old house, surrounded by old families who'd lived here for generations, several miles from Williamsburg. It would take an hour or longer to get to Richmond or Norfolk, and neither city was exactly the hub of the world.

"I'm still thinking about it. It's a great place to live and would be wonderful for children."

He bit a savage bite from the cookie. "There's a lot more in life than children," he said.

She looked at him and shrugged. "Jake, let's not fight over anything. Let's enjoy this Christmas. For all the things that might have been, let's give ourselves a terrific memory to last all our lives."

"Why?"

"Why not?"

He studied her for a moment. "Why the change of heart? Yesterday you ordered me out."

She licked her lips. "I was thinking we don't have a lot of memories since we haven't spent a lot of time together. Don't you think one day you'll regret not having a family, not spending time with that family? Careers are fine but are not supposed to be so consuming people don't have time for other things."

He didn't look ahead that far. One day he'd be too old to investigate the news in foreign locales. Maybe too old to work at all. What would he do then? Thinking back to the past didn't figure in his plans. But if he was alone, wouldn't it be something to have one special memory of the girl he'd loved enough to marry six years ago? He'd failed her, he knew. But that was something else he couldn't change. Maybe Cath was right, take the gift of a perfect Christmas and treasure the memory all the rest of his life.

He wasn't willing to concede he'd be alone. There had to be some way he could reach her, show her they belonged together. Convince her to stay with him.

If they had the best Christmas ever, wouldn't that sway Cath they were good together? Make her see they shouldn't throw away what they had on a nebulous future which might not include that huge family she was always talking about.

"We can give it a try," he said, already coming up with ideas to change his wife's mind and keep their marriage intact. Wasn't Christmas the time of miracles? He'd need one to keep Cath, and he was way overdue to receive a miracle.

She poured the cider into mugs and went to sit at the table, handing Jake one.

"I forgot to ask you earlier if you'd check on the battle of Kings Mountain for me. I saw mention of it in the journal I'm reading."

"Know who wrote it?"

"Tansy. Her husband was Jonathan. I'm guessing Williamson, since Aunt Sally said that her family had owned the house since it was built. She never married. I guess it came down through the sons, but don't really know. You'd think I'd know more about my family history."

"Most people don't know much beyond the relatives they actually knew. We can look up on the Internet if you like. I brought my laptop."

"Naturally," she said dryly. Then wrinkled her nose. "That was tacky. Of course you'd have your laptop. Thanks for the offer. Aunt Sally didn't have a computer and I'd hate to wait until I return home. I want to know about the war. And if Jonathan came home."

"Doesn't the journal say?" he asked.

"I'm reading a day at a time. She wrote several pages each day." Cath toyed with her mug for a moment, darting another glance at Jake.

"In a way, I'm seeing some of myself in her journal. She's home alone—here I guess—and missing her husband. It must have been hard to be a woman back then with her husband gone. She mentions neighbors helping out with some of the farm chores. I think Jonathan had been gone for months."

"Some men were gone years. Some went to fight except when they had to return home for harvest. It was a rag-tag army at best."

"She was so lonely. I wish I knew how old she was. Sounds like she and Jonathan hadn't been married that long."

"Maybe there're other journals."

"I hope so. I wanted to look in the trunk again. Maybe I missed another one. It was mostly full of clothes, so another journal could have slid down."

"We can look tomorrow."

"What about cleaning?"

"How long will it take to look through a few boxes to see if there are other journals? You remember where the trunk was?"

She nodded. Right by that old cradle. Had it been Tansy and Jonathan's?

"Then look in nearby boxes, chances are stuff is stored by age. There sure doesn't seem to be any other method to the storage."

"Mmm." Cath sipped her cider, wondering about Tansy and the past and how closely she felt tied to the woman. Was history repeating itself with a slight twist? Jake wasn't going to war to fight, but he was away for long periods of time, and usually reporting on armed conflicts.

"I'm tired. I'm going up to bed for good now," she said, rising a little later.

He followed her to the foot of the stairs.

"I'm glad you came back down to decorate the tree," he said.

"Me, too. It's pretty, isn't it?" she asked, looking at it through the archway. It sparkled and shimmered with lights and ornaments.

"We didn't get any tinsel on it," she said.

"It doesn't need it. Good night, Cath."

He kissed her briefly and headed to the living room. He'd clean up the boxes and other clutter and then head for bed. Tomorrow he'd begin his campaign.

Cath awoke with a feeling of anticipation. She and Jake had reached a truce last night. They'd enjoy each other's company for the next couple of days, and then separate. It would be nice to have someone to share the holidays with. And with this new truce, there'd be no pushing to change her decision.

She frowned. At least she hoped so. The kisses he'd given her last night didn't seem as platonic as they could be. But he'd been away for a long time. What was a kiss or two between friends?

Could they be friends? She tried to picture them meeting for dinner or something each time he returned to the States. She could not picture them reminiscing together.

There was too much between them, including that flare of attraction and awareness that rose every time he came near her. Just lying in her bed she felt fluttery merely thinking about Jake. God she wished things were different and that he'd be home for her every night!

Pushing aside her confused thoughts, she rose and quickly dressed. Despite the heater, it was still cold in the bedrooms. One glance out the window showed a storm was brewing. The intermittent sunshine of yesterday was gone. Gray skies made the day seem dreary. There would probably be rain by afternoon, she thought.

Wearing old jeans and a sweatshirt, she went downstairs. The house was silent. The Christmas tree lights had been turned on, sparkling in the pale morning light. Jake was already up.

But when she went into the kitchen, he wasn't there. The coffee was warm on the stove. The box of Christmas cookies was on the table. Had that been his breakfast? She looked out the window to see if he was on one of his walks and spotted him near the river. He seemed to like walking along the bank. It must be so peaceful and serene after the places he'd visited.

Still, wasn't he cold? The branches on the trees swayed in the wind. She looked at the sky again, ominous in its grayness. Would it snow? She wished she had a radio to keep up with the weather forecasts. Aunt Sally hadn't had a radio, only an old television set that was on its last legs the last time Cath visited. She hadn't seen a new one since she'd been here. The old one was in

Aunt Sally's bedroom—not a place she was going with Jake ensconced there.

Pouring herself a cup of coffee, she watched Jake. He stood near the edge of the bank, a short drop to the river. She almost called out to be careful. What if he slipped or tripped and fell into the icy river?

Then she almost laughed. How foolish. The man practically lived in danger zones. What was a riverbank?

He turned and walked with his head bent, pausing and then stooping down. She could not see what he was doing, but watched until he stood. He glanced at the house. Could he see her at the window?

Cath turned quickly and went to the refrigerator to pull out some eggs. She'd prepare a big breakfast, mainly for him, and then get ready to plunge into the cleaning she had scheduled.

By midmorning, Jake has received two calls, each pulling him away from the tasks at hand. They'd started on the room across from the one he was using as soon as breakfast was finished. They worked well together and the task went quickly, despite the interruptions.

"Another room?" Jake asked as they left that one, cleaning supplies in hand.

"Not today. After I shower and fix lunch, I want to use the laptop to see what I can find out about the war. Maybe even find mention of Jonathan. I suppose his last name was Williamson. But it could have been a different one that many generations ago."

"I have a couple of calls to make this after-noon, so you can be searching for your long lost kin while I work."

She bit her lip. Was this when he'd get a new assignment and be off? Would he leave before Christmas? It was two days away. Even if some-thing was happening that needed reporting, surely Jake could stay for two more days. Let someone else cover the news.

When had she gone from wishing him not there to hoping he'd stay another two days?

CHAPTER SIX

CATH settled in the living room with Jake's laptop. The lights still shone from the tree. Looking out the window, she was surprised to see light snowflakes drifting down. She'd known a storm was brewing, but hadn't expected snow. So it might be a white Christmas, she mused.

She spent the next couple of hours researching the War for Independence, noting major southern battles, searching for Jonathan Williamson. There was no record of a soldier by that name that she found, but she was fascinated about the accounts of the different skirmishes.

"Find anything?" Jake asked, standing in the doorway. He'd been on the phone the entire time. She'd heard the murmur of his voice coming from the kitchen.

"Lots of information, nothing on a Jonathan Williamson from Virginia. Are you finished your calls?"

"For the time being."

"No major story needing your reporting?" she asked, stretching out her legs. She was feeling a bit stiff from sitting for two hours in front of the computer after all the bending she'd done while cleaning.

"No." He walked over to one of the front windows and looked out. "It's snowing heavier now than before," he said.

She put the computer on the table and rose to join him. Several inches of snow blanketed the yard and trees. She shivered, not really cold, but feeling the chill from the air near the glass.

"You have the only television in your room," she said. "Check the news to see what to expect."

"Or look it up on the Internet," he said.

She complied and found the forecast more

severe than she'd expected. "It says we could have more than a foot of snow. And the cold weather is due to continue through the week, so it's not going to melt anytime soon."

"Do we need to go anywhere?"

Cath shook her head, staring at the five-day forecast on the computer. She'd bought enough food to last a week or longer. She had made sure she bought all she needed for a nice Christmas dinner. It wouldn't be a hardship to remain inside.

"I wish we had some wood for a fire," she said wistfully, shutting down the computer.

"There's some stacked beside the barn."

"Carriage house," she corrected absently. "Is there? Do you suppose it'll burn?"

"It's been there at least since last summer, probably longer. It'll be nice and dry. I'll bring some in."

"I'll help."

They bundled up and went out into the snow. Cath lifted her head to the falling flakes, delighting in the feel of them landing on her cheeks. She laughed and spun around.

"This is so much fun. Usually I hate having it snow, because I have to go to work and know the streets are going to be treacherous. But this is different. No responsibilities until January. It can snow all week!"

He watched her with a brooding gaze. "If it snowed all week, we'd have ten feet of snow to plow through at the end."

"You know what I mean. Isn't this fun?"

"It beats the dry heat of the Middle East," he said. "Come on, the wood is on the far side."

They brought in several armfuls of split logs, stacking them near the large fireplace. Then Jake found a tarp in the carriage house and covered the rest of the pile so it wouldn't get wet with the snow.

"Isn't that a little late?" Cath asked, watching him. "There's already snow sticking."

"But it's not much and we may end up needing this for heat if something happens to the power.

This will keep any more snow from accumulating directly on the wood."

"Want to walk along the river?" Cath asked, not ready to go back inside. She'd seen him several times along the bank of the river. What was the appeal? In the muted light, the water looked gray and cold as it silently flowed on its way to the sea.

"Until our feet get cold," he said.

"We should have brought boots."

"I wasn't expecting to come at all," he reminded her. Taking her hand in his, he gestured upstream. "Let's go this way, I haven't explored this direction."

The snow made walking treacherous. They stayed well away from the riverbank, slipping and skidding from time to time as they trudged along in the quiet of the afternoon.

Soon they passed another house, lights blazing from the downstairs windows, necessary with the storm darkening the sky.

"Do you know who lives there?" Jake asked.

"Mrs. Watson. She was one of Aunt Sally's favorite friends, though she was younger by a decade or more. When I visited, she'd often have us over for dinner. Other than Mrs. Watson and the McDonalds, Aunt Sally devoted herself to me and didn't visit with her friends or neighbors while I was staying with her. The McDonalds were the family on the other side who had the boat I used."

The next house they walked behind was dark. No one home, obviously. "The Carstairs live here. Wonder if they've gone off for the holidays."

Some time later Cath stopped. "My feet are freezing." She was getting cold all over, except for her hand held by Jake. Her hair was covered with snow, as was Jake's. She shook her head, dislodging a shower of flakes. Shivering in the cold air, she noticed the wind seemed to have picked up.

"Time to return anyway," Jake said. "Can you feel the wind?"

She nodded.

They hurried back to the house. Entering the

kitchen, Cath toed off her shoes, wiggling her toes against the linoleum floor. "It feels so much warmer in here."

"Want to get that fire going now, or later?" Jake asked, shrugging out of his jacket.

Once again Cath wondered if it were warm enough for him. She should have thought of that before suggesting the walk.

"Now's fine, I guess. What are we going to do the rest of the afternoon?" It was too early to start supper, but Cath wasn't sure she just wanted to sit in the living room together and talk.

"We could explore the cellar a bit more," he said, hanging both their jackets across the back of two chairs to let them drip on the floor as the snow melted. "Look for those journals you want to find."

"Okay." Cath wasn't as excited about exploring the cellar as Jake seemed, but she knew she'd much rather have him with her than do it on her own. Maybe in addition to searching for the journals, she could make a hasty inventory and get some idea of what would be involved in clearing the place.

On the other hand, if she did decide to remain, she would have years ahead of her in which to go through the items in the cellar and determine what to keep and what to discard.

She grabbed a tablet and pencil and headed down the steps after Jake. He seemed to relish the idea of wandering through the spooky place. Halfway down the door slammed behind her.

"Did you leave a window open?" Jake asked from the bottom of the stairs.

"No, but that door slams shut a lot. I forgot to prop it open. I think the house slants or something," she said, descending the remaining stairs. "When you think about it, a house that's two hundred years old and still standing is pretty remarkable."

"There speaks a child of modern America. I've been places where dwellings are several hundred years old, not just two."

"Mmm." She looked around. The dim lighting faintly illuminated the clutter. "Where do we start?"

"It's your cellar, where did you find the journal?"

"Over here." She retraced her steps from earlier and soon stopped by the old cradle. Nudging it, she watched it rock gently for a couple of moments. "I wonder how old this is? It's probably been in the family for generations."

Jake looked at the cradle, the tightness in his chest returning. Did all roads lead to children? A sadness swept through him. He wished he could see Cath when she was pregnant. See her holding a newborn, her head bent over him, her blond hair shielding her face. Then she'd look up and he'd see the love shining in her eyes.

Like he used to see it shining for him. Couldn't Cath see what they had was good? How could she throw it all away?

"Probably has dry rot," he said. He looked over the area. Other furniture was haphazardly stacked out of the narrow aisle. There were trunks and crates and boxes stacked two and three high.

"It does not have dry rot and with a little cleaning and polish it'll be beautiful. Carry it upstairs for me, would you?"

"Whatever for?" He looked at her.

"I can clean it up while I'm here."

"Cath—" He had nothing to say. It had all been said. "Fine." He pulled it away from the other furniture and lifted it. It was heavier than he expected and awkward, but he maneuvered it through the narrow space and to the bottom of the stairs. "Get the door," he said, motioning her to go ahead of him.

She passed him and ran up the steps.

"It's stuck," she said, pushing against it.

"Great." He set down the cradle and, skipping every other step, joined Cath at the top. He tried the door. It didn't budge.

"It didn't lock, did it?" he asked, twisting the knob.

"No. It sticks sometimes."

He pushed it with his shoulder. There wasn't enough room on the top step to get much leverage. Jake tried again. The solid door held firm.

He looked around the frame. "The hinges are on the other side, but maybe I can pry off the board on this side and get to them."

Just then the electricity failed and they were plunged into darkness.

"Jake?" Cath reached out and clutched his arm.

He turned and drew her closer. "It's all right. Just be careful and don't fall down the stairs. I guess the storm got worse."

"This place gives me the creeps," she said.

"It's only the underside of the house. Come on, take the stairs slowly and we'll get to the bottom. Do you know if your aunt had any flashlights or candles down here?"

"I haven't a clue. I never came here much when I was a kid. I know there are candles in the drawer in the kitchen."

"Fat lot of good they do us right now."

"Can't you pry off the frame and get the door open?"

"Sure. It may take a little longer in the dark, but we'll manage." He wasn't sure how, but she sounded nervous. He said what he could to ease her mind.

They reached the bottom, as Jake found out when his shins connected with the cradle. "Dammit," he muttered. If Cath had let the fool thing stay where she found it…

"So how can you work on the door when you can't see anything?" she asked, still holding tightly to his arm. "And where are you going to find any tools. I bet Aunt Sally had them all in the carriage house."

"If we can find a screwdriver or some kind of metal wedge to pry off the board surrounding the door, we'll be all set. There has to be something around here."

"I don't know where anything is in this place," she said. "How can you find anything in the dark?"

"Then we'll just sit down and wait for the

power outage to end. It might not be long. Probably not as long as some of the places I've been."

"Or it could last a day or two," Cath said.

"Don't borrow trouble."

They sat on the bottom step. Jake looked off into the darkness. His eyes would have adjusted by now to any light. There was none. He could try to find some device that would work, but not knowing the layout, or what was even available, it sounded like a fool's errand. Plus, if Cath didn't turn loose his arm, he wasn't going anywhere.

He pried her fingers off, then laced them with his. "There's nothing to be scared about," he said. "It's just old furniture and boxes of stuff."

"Maybe ghosts."

He laughed. "I doubt it. Your aunt Sally lived here all her life, she'd have told you if there were any ghosts."

"Maybe."

"Tell me about Tansy. Isn't that the name of the woman who wrote that journal you're captivated by?" he said, hoping to get her mind off her fear. "She may have been in this cellar herself."

"I wonder who she was. And what happened to them."

"How far have you read?"

"Just a couple of entries. They're lengthy, as if she had lots of time on her hands and poured her feelings out on the page. She talks about neighbors, and the cold, and trying to get the farm chores done on her own. I sometimes feel—"

Jake could tell she was holding something back. "What? There's more to it, surely," he said.

"She was lonely and afraid for her husband," Cath said in a soft voice. "It's uncanny how her words reflect my own feelings."

"What?" That startled him.

"Did you think I never worried about you when you were gone? You don't exactly have a routine, boring job, Jake. You put yourself in danger all the time and never give a thought to how those of us back home feel."

"Who else would care?" he asked.

"I bet your mother does," she said.

"Don't go there, Cath," he warned. He rarely thought about his mother. That was in the past and he planned for it to stay there. Cath knew he had nothing to do with his family, and why. Cath was all he needed.

For a moment he wondered what would happen if she went through with her plan of divorce. He couldn't imagine finding another woman to spend his life with.

"Okay, then we'll leave your mother out of it and talk about me. Us. You wanted to know why I want a divorce. Imagine the roles were reversed and I went to Bosnia in the midst of fighting, or to an earthquake area where the building codes are so laughable that the mildest aftershock topples whole buildings. No guarantees of safety. You wouldn't worry?"

Jake nodded, then remembered she couldn't see in the dark. "Of course I'd worry, especially someone like you."

"Leave that aside. I understand you think you're

invincible, but you're not. Terrible things happen
to journalists. So that's one part. The other is the
loneliness. Jake, I don't like living alone. I don't
like having no one to share my day with, or make
plans for the weekend, or just talk about friends
and co-workers. I miss having someone there to
talk over situations that are new and different, to
get some ideas for dealing with problem children,
or gifted ones. I'm tired of sandwiches for dinner,
but don't want to cook for one."

"I'm not a teacher," he said. "I can't stay in
one place and do my job, Cath. You know that."

"That was an example. Honestly, you're not
trying to see my side of it."

"I'm lonely, too, Cath," he confessed.

"Then why, for heaven's sake, aren't you
home living with me?"

"You know my job—"

"No! Stop! I do not want to hear a word about
your job. I want to hear about you. Why aren't
we sharing a home, making a family, building
a life together?"

"How do you propose I support this family if I don't report the news?" He was starting to get mad. Why was he the one at fault? She could travel with him. Granted, not to a war zone or disaster area. But she could move to London or Rome and be closer to where he usually worked. It would be easier for him to get to London than Washington.

"I don't have a suggestion, but I do think that's the crux of the matter. You like your job and it isn't in Washington. Or here. I'm growing to love this house. I don't know the neighbors, but maybe I'll make an effort to meet them and see if I could fit in. I think a complete break and change would be good," she said.

He hoped he wasn't hearing things that weren't there, he could swear he heard an undertone of sadness in her voice. Was there a chance she really didn't want to end their marriage? If so, she had a funny way of showing it.

"What changed?" he asked. "We've been married six years. What changed, Cath?"

"Aunt Sally's death made me look at things differently, I think. I only saw her a few times a year even though Washington isn't that far away. I should have visited more often. Having flying visits from you isn't enough. I see friends and co-workers going home to families each night, and I go home to an empty condo. I'm not getting any younger. If I want to find another man, to have a family, I need to do something now. I don't want to be old like my parents were when I have a child. I want to enjoy each stage of development from baby to toddler to teenager."

"You're around children all day," he said.

"Other people's children. And only a few hours a day. I don't hear the stories at the dinner table about what they learned in school, or what their best friend said. I don't make cookies or Halloween costumes, or Christmas decorations. It was hard being the only child of older parents. I want what I have never had."

"It's overrated," he grumbled.

"You should want what you never had, Jake.

You said your mother turned to her new children by her second husband, virtually ignoring you. You missed as much as I did growing up. Maybe it was even worse since you witnessed it but couldn't participate."

"Don't psychoanalyze me, Cath. I did fine, got out as soon as I was eighteen. My mother is welcome to her second family."

"You know she was wrong to ignore you, or let your stepfather have the influence he had. You would make a great father—if you were home. You'd remember what your real father did and follow his example. But it's never going to happen, is it, Jake? We've been through this a dozen times before. You have your job and I have my dreams and they don't mesh."

He turned to her, finding her head in the darkness and covering her lips with his. This part of their marriage had always worked. She responded as she always did. Her kiss was warm and welcoming and so at odds with the words she spoke. This wasn't a woman who wanted to leave her marriage; he couldn't believe that. Yet if something didn't change, and soon, she'd follow through with her plan.

Could he show her how much they meant to each other?

His hands skimmed over her shoulders down to her back, pulling her into his lap and deeper into the embrace. She was like liquid silk, warm and pliant and sweet. He murmured words of wanting in her ear, brushing kisses against her cheeks, trailing them to her throat, feeling the rapid pulse at the base.

Her arms tightened around him, and he felt her breasts press against his chest. If the cellar wasn't cold and dusty, he'd make love to her here and now. He'd been gone too long. And it looked as if his strategy was backfiring on him. He didn't know if Cath was softening, but he wanted her more than ever. He couldn't bear the thought of her walking away forever. Yet the ending seemed inevitable. Why hadn't he seen that from the beginning?

"Hello, anyone home?" a faint voice called.

Jake and Cath sprang apart, turning as one to the door at the top of the stairs.

"Wait here," he said, standing and setting her on her feet. He climbed the stairs and pounded on the door. "We're trapped in the cellar. Are you in the house?"

"Dear me, I came to use your phone." The voice came from an elderly woman.

"I'll run home and get my nephew, maybe he can help."

Less than five minutes later Jake heard footsteps in the kitchen. Someone rattled the handle of the door.

"Is it locked?" a man asked.

"No, stuck only. I've tried pushing from this side," Jake said.

"Hold on. I've got hold of the handle. You push and I'll pull."

For several seconds they tried but the door wouldn't budge.

"Can you see the hinges?" Jake called.

"Sure. They look old as can be. Let me find something to pry them off," the man answered.

"There're tools in the carriage house," Cath called.

Within ten minutes the man had the hinges off and together he and Jake were able to pry open the door. The stranger lifted it out of the way as Cath scrambled up the steps, glad to escape the cellar. She'd never again complain about the dim lighting—it was much better than total darkness.

"Thank you!" she exclaimed when she stepped into the kitchen.

An elderly woman and a handsome young man stood looking at her.

"You're welcome, Cath dear. I thought you'd come to visit me before now. How have you been?" the woman asked.

"I've been fine, Mrs. Watson. And we've been so busy cleaning and clearing out things I haven't had a chance to do any visiting. I'm glad to see you." Cath gave her a quick hug and then smiled at the young man beside her.

"This is my nephew, staying with me for Christmas. Bart Butler."

"Jake Morgan." Jake extended his hand and they shook. "And my wife, Cath."

"Sally and I were neighbors for more than forty years. I sure do miss her. I remember how very fond of you she was. Calling you the granddaughter she never had," Mrs. Watson told Cath.

She nodded, remembering her aunt telling her that. She considered Cath's father the child she never had, and had doted on him as well.

"My goodness, I came to see if you had a phone that worked. Mine is dead and I need to call to refill a prescription before Christmas," Pearl said. "I told Bart I could manage on my own in the snow, but didn't expect to find that door stuck. Sally used to say she was going to get it fixed. I guess she never got around to it."

"My cell works," Jake said, nodding to the kitchen counter where he'd left it. From now on, he'd keep it with him.

"I appreciate that," Bart said. "I don't mind

driving into town, but if they can't fill it or there's a problem, I'd hate to drive all the way in this weather for nothing."

"Glad you needed the phone. We couldn't see a thing in the dark and I was wondering how we'd get out," Jake said, handing his phone to Mrs. Watson.

"We could have been stuck there all night," Cath said with a shiver. "I should have come over when I first arrived to tell you I was staying for Christmas."

"We saw the lights, so we knew you were here," Bart said as his aunt spoke on the phone. "I saw you out walking earlier. Too cold for me."

"You're not from here?" Cath asked.

"I live in Richmond. But I'm spending the holidays with my aunt this year. She didn't want to come to Richmond."

"No other family?" Jake asked.

"A boatload. My folks are taking a cruise this year, however. And two of my sisters are taking their families skiing. My brother and his wife are spending Christmas with her folks this year, so I was on my own. Aunt Pearl thought it better for me to come visit her than for her to visit me. I think she had some concern on the ability of a bachelor to fix a suitable Christmas meal."

Jake didn't like the smile Cath gave the man. Was she already sizing up Bart Butler as a candidate for her next husband? How convenient that would be, living right next door to Sally's house.

"There, it's all taken care of, dear," Mrs. Watson said to her nephew. "They'll even deliver tomorrow, even though it's Christmas Eve. So you don't have to drive in the snow."

"Good." He smiled at his aunt. "Not that I wouldn't have gone for you."

"I know, dear. We'd best be going back. It is colder than I thought it would be."

"Thanks for rescuing us," Cath said.

"Anytime," Bart said, turning his smile in Cath's direction.

"Do you have any idea how long the power will be out?" she asked.

"Not a clue. If our phone worked, we could have called the power company. They usually can estimate when it'll be restored. You can call, if you want to get an estimate," Bart said.

"Wait while I check." Cath retrieved Jake's phone and looked for the phone book. She remembered Jake's finding the Christmas Tree Farm in the book, and leaving it on the dining room table.

The power company estimated electricity would be restored within two hours. It would be full dark by then as it was already after four.

"Will you two be all right?" Pearl asked.

"Of course," Jake said, putting a proprietary arm across Cath's shoulders. He didn't need any more attention from the neighbors, especially Bart.

"Aunt Sally had oil lamps and we'll light them if we need light," Cath said.

"There's a gas stove, so you'll be able to cook," Pearl said, glancing around the kitchen. "Or you are both welcome to come over to our house for supper."

"We'll manage," Jake said.

"We'll be fine. Thank you for inviting us. I hope to see you again before I return to Washington," Cath said graciously, nudging Jake surreptitiously in the ribs.

"Oh, dear, you're leaving after the holidays? We were hoping you were going to stay. This house seems so lonely when no one is here," Pearl said.

"We live in Washington," Jake said firmly.

"Actually, I'm thinking of moving here next summer," Cath said, slipping from under his arm and moving closer to Pearl. "I'm a teacher. Do you think I'd have a chance of finding a job around here?"

"Sure thing," Bart said with a broad smile. "The area is growing and new schools need teachers. Aunt Pearl knows a couple of people on the school board, maybe she could put in a good word. It'd be nice for her to have a close neighbor again. The family on the other side of her house only visits on weekends."

Jake could imagine how nice Pearl would find it. Or was Bart more concerned about when *he* visited?

"No decisions have been made," he said, glaring at Cath. For every step forward, she seemed determined to take one back.

CHAPTER SEVEN

WHEN Mrs. Watson and her nephew left, Jake turned to study the door. The old house had settled over the years, and the door frame was no longer square. He had enough basic skills to plane the door so it would fit better, and shaving a bit of wood from it would insure it wouldn't stick shut again. Bart had offered to help, but he didn't need the young neighbor's assistance.

Jake planned to fix it right away if he could find the proper tools. He didn't like thinking what might have happened to Cath if she'd been caught down there alone with no neighbors needing the phone.

"If you're going to fix that now, could you bring up the cradle first?" Cath asked.

Jake nodded and brought it up. He placed it gently down in the center of the kitchen. It was old, yet had obviously been cared for through the years. How many babies had slept in its shelter? Cath's eyes were shining as she gazed at it. He felt a pang. Once she'd looked at him that way. Would she ever do so again?

"I'm going to the garage to see if there're any tools I can use to fix the door. It's too cold to let the cellar air come up into this level if we don't have to," he said.

Maybe he couldn't bring that shine to her eyes again, but he could keep her safe.

Cath nodded, already reaching for the rags she'd used for cleaning. She'd wipe down the cradle, give it a good polish to see what it looked like. Maybe there was even a small mattress for it somewhere and some bedding, though she couldn't imagine who had been the last baby to use it. Had it been her father? She didn't believe she herself had ever been put in it as her parents hadn't visited often, preferring Sally to come to their house.

The simple carving on the headboard was of flowers. She worked to get all the dust out of the crevasses and corners, wondering who had made it, who had done the carving. A proud father-to-be, she was sure. Maybe even Jonathan?

Jake returned with a handful of tools. He moved the door, placing it half on the table, half on the back of two chairs and started shaving curlicues of wood from the edge. Working on their respective projects kept both from feeling chilled in the cooling air. They'd really need the fire in a while if the electricity didn't come back on. While the heater was oil fueled, it needed electricity to work.

Cath brought out the wood wax she'd seen beneath the sink and began to work it into the old wood. Once finished, she sat back on her heels and smiled. The cradle was a beautiful piece of furniture. It was worn a bit on the sides, as if by many arms reaching in to pick up an infant, but that made it all the more special. The carving was as sharp and clear as if it had been done yesterday.

She pushed it to set it rocking. It continued on its own for several moments. How safe and secure it would hold a baby. Would one of her children sleep in it? She looked over to where Jake worked on the door. Together they'd make the world's most perfect baby. If he'd only be there for her.

Cath rose, cleaned up and pulled some milk from the refrigerator. "Want some hot chocolate?" she asked as Jake patiently shaved another thin sliver of wood from the door. "It's getting cold in here."

"Sure. I'm almost done. Then we can go into the living room and build that fire."

She put the pan on the gas stove and slowly heated it. She glanced from time to time at Jake, feeling odd. It was so domestic, wife in the kitchen fixing something for them both, husband working on a project. How many times had they'd done something like this? Too few. Looking around the old kitchen she could imagine Tansy preparing something for her Jonathan. Instead of the gas range Cath used, Tansy might have had a woodstove, or even an open hearth. Had Jonathan sat in the warm kitchen, lovingly carving the cradle with flowers and designs for a baby's arrival? The modern kitchen faded and for a moment Cath could imagine how it might have looked two hundred years ago.

"Is it still snowing?" Jake asked.

Cath started, then looked out the window. "Yes." She had better pay attention so the milk didn't boil over. In only a couple of minutes, she had two large mugs of chocolate topped with whipped cream. She carried Jake's to him. He brushed her fingers when he took the mug and looked deep into her eyes.

"Thanks," he said. Taking a sip, he never let his gaze waiver.

Cath felt the touch almost like a shock. She returned his regard, lost in the dark brown of his eyes, the message clear. He wanted her. With effort she tore her gaze away.

"It'll be dark before long. Do you think I should get the oil lamps out and make sure they have fuel?" she asked, feeling flustered. She could almost grasp the tangible desire that flooded through her. She had loved Jake so much when they first married. In many ways, nothing had changed.

"It wouldn't hurt. Even if the power comes back, there's nothing saying it won't go out again later," he said, sipping the hot beverage.

"Better have candles in each room, then, with matches so we'd have light to get to the lamps," Cath said, glad for something to do. The spell was broken. She needed to remember to keep her distance.

The lamps were right where she remembered. Opening the cupboard she took stock of everything stored in them. She planned to leave the cleaning of the kitchen until last, able to make better inroads into the bedrooms and other rooms of the house first. If this cabinet was any indication, the room would take days to sort through and organize. Cath mentally revised her schedule. With both the cellar and kitchen ahead, not to mention the carriage house, there was truly no way she could complete everything this holiday.

Maybe she'd come down for the next few weekends and keep plugging away at the tasks. That way she'd be finished before summer.

It wouldn't be the same with Jake gone, she thought, taking down the lamps and setting them on the counter. She had planned to work alone, but his arrival had changed that. Now she couldn't imagine doing all this on her own. What if she'd been caught in the cellar alone? What if Mrs. Watson had not needed to use the phone?

Taking down three lamps, she washed the

globes. Then she raised the wick on each. Still plenty of oil in the base and the wicks looked trimmed. Lighting them, she soon had a bright, steady glow from each lamp.

"They work," she said just as the heater gave an *umph* and the lights came on in the cellar.

"Your timing is perfect. Maybe you should have lit them earlier," Jake teased.

"Maybe." She blew them out and put them on one side of the counter, just in case.

She glanced at the clock. It wasn't yet six o'clock.

"Do you think I have time to bake some cookies?"

"Why not, we're not on any schedule. And a warm oven will help bring up the temperature in this room."

Cath wasn't sure why she had a sudden desire to bake, must be the housework, nesting. Or maybe it was she wanted to do something for Jake, fatten him up while he was with her, so she felt she was doing something. She began to mix the ingredients for shortbread cookies. They were his favorite.

"There, I think that'll work," Jake said, sanding the edge of the door lightly, then wiping off the dust. "Help me put it back in place."

They rehung the door and it swung closed. She turned the knob and the door opened easily. Letting it go, it once again slammed shut. Again she opened it with no effort.

"That's perfect. Thanks," she said.

He gathered the tools and started for the carriage house. "I'll sweep up the mess when I get back."

"I can manage that," Cath said, "you did all the work." She quickly swept up the wood chips and sawdust and moved the cradle to the back wall, out of the way. The first batch of cookies was ready to come from the oven. She put in another batch.

Some time later Cath realized Jake hadn't come back from the carriage house. What was he doing out there? She glanced out the window, but the angle was wrong. All she could see was the river and the edge of the old building. He wasn't standing on the banks like she'd seen him before. Was he still in the carriage house?

Jake leaned against the back door of the carriage house and stared at the slow-moving river. He didn't see the silvery water as it drifted by, nor the snow that softly drifted from the sky. He was miles away in thought. It felt as if he was trying to hold a slippery eel or something. The tighter he held on, the more Cath seemed to slip away.

He wasn't ready to go back inside. Yet it was too cold and wet to walk along the river. So his choice was to stand here and freeze. He turned back into the carriage house. Another place needing to be cleaned. Had Cath allowed for that in her schedule? He walked around the old structure. It had gaps in the walls, but the roof looked sound. Obviously a catch-all place, it was stacked with boxes and old furniture. Either there'd been no more room in the cellar, or this furniture wasn't as treasured.

He spied an old carriage in one corner, too dilapidated to use. Once horses had pulled that carriage, maybe taking the Williamsons into Williamsburg or even as far as Richmond. Walking over, he noticed how the barrel springs sagged, and how the spokes to the high wheels were broken in spots, making the carriage sag at an odd angle. Everything was covered in a thick layer of dust. The conveyance looked to be from the late 1800s, not that he was an expert on old carriages. He tried moving it, but feared the wheels would collapse after budging it only a little and having them creak in protest.

He kicked the dirt. Dry as dust. At least the weather was kept from the place. Glancing around, he saw signs of deterioration of the old building. It was not as in good a shape as the house. The gaps in the walls let the elements in if the wind blew in the right direction. He turned to head to the house when he spotted a small sliver of metal jutting up near the carriage wheel. The small movement of the carriage must have dislodged the dirt to reveal it. He looked closer, then scraped away some of the dirt and uncovered a small metal box. Had it deliberately been hidden, or had it fallen and been covered by dirt over the years?

Taking it to the workbench on the far side, he brushed off the accumulated dirt. The fastener was rusted. He tried to pry it open, then broke the latch to lift the lid. Inside were several coins and a gold pendant on a chain. Lifting it, he saw it was a locket, letters entwined on one side. How long had it been buried? To whom had it belonged, and why had it never been recovered?

"More mysteries for Cath to unravel," he murmured. He examined the coins, gold with an eagle on one side. Jake was startled to find the dates stamped on them from the 1850s. There were also two Confederate coins. Someone's treasure hidden from marauding Yankee troops?

He put them in his pocket, knowing they'd make the perfect Christmas surprise for Cath. She loved old things, and to get such a treasure from her own property would be special. He still lived with the fantasy of seeing her in that sexy nightie he'd bought. Maybe wearing this gold locket in the firelight.

Cath took out the last batch of cookies, setting them on a rack to cool. Where was Jake? She peered out the kitchen window again, but didn't see him. She was starting to get concerned. His jacket wasn't thick and it was cold enough inside to give her an idea of how cold it was outside. Should she go look for him?

She opened the back door. From there she could see into the carriage house. Jake was at the workbench, bending over something. She hoped he had enough sense to come in out of the cold before he caught a chill or something.

Reassured he was fine, she went into the living room. It still felt cool, despite the efforts of the heater. The fire they'd started earlier had died down. She added logs and stirred it to get it going again.

Feeling restless, she considered what to do. Maybe she'd read some more of Tansy's journal. Their expedition to search for more books had been aborted and she wasn't anxious to go back down in the cellar again. Next time, she'd make sure they carried flashlights. Of course the door wouldn't jam again, but she didn't want to be caught in the far corner if the power failed.

Or she could use Jake's computer to try to find out more about Jonathan Williamson. Had he fought in other battles leading up to Yorktown?

She watched as the logs flared and began to give off some heat. Satisfied the fire would warm things up, she turned on the laptop and began to search for more about the war Jonathan fought in. Knowing she had a great-great-grandfather fight changed how she viewed history.

A short time later she gave up on the war and

began to look for Web sites describing life in the 1700s in America. Some were geared for elementary school level and she loved the sketches of clothes, houses, cooking utensils and early carriages. Maybe she'd make a special project for her kids when school started again.

The more she read, the more she appreciated the fine work that had gone into building the house, built before modern equipment. Two hundred years later it was still housing a member of the Williamson family.

Impatient to find out what happened to Tansy and Jonathan, she turned off the computer and went to find the journal.

The next entry began:

Tomorrow is Christmas,. It has begun to snow in earnest. Everything is covered and I hope my chickens survive. It is unusually cold. If I don't get the eggs right when they are laid, they could be frozen. It's hard to walk to the chicken coop, but I have a rope to use as a guide. Still no word from my husband. I hope he is planning a wonderful surprise and will show up tonight before I retire. I would so welcome another night in his arms. And Christmas won't be a special day without him here.

I miss my family. Maybe I should have gone to stay with my parents, but I could not bear the thought of Jonathan making his way home and not finding me here.

Cath gave a start. That was what she'd done, left home when Jake said he'd made a monumental effort to get home for the holidays. She bit her lip in remorse. She should have at least let him know where she was.

Jake had figured it out. Jonathan would surely have known if his wife wasn't home that she'd be with her parents. How sweet of Tansy to wait alone and lonely in hopes of her husband's arrival.

Everything in the house is ready. I have boughs of holly decorating the rooms, and a yule log ready for the fireplace. I have mulled the cider, which fills the house with a delicious fragrance. I do hope I don't have to drink it all by myself. I'm sure several neighbors will stop by to wish me a happy Christmas in the afternoon. Last year Jonathan and I drove to friends and neighbors to raise a glass of cheer. It was so festive. I never suspected we wouldn't do it this year as well. Maybe we shall, if only he gets home soon.

The entry ended abruptly.

Cath felt a frisson of dread as she turned the page. In stark letters the words—

Jonathan is dead. How will I go on?

The paper was smudged, as if by tears.

Cath's heart dropped. Slowly she ran her fingers over the long-dried tears. What happened? The entry contained only those blunt words, no date, no details, nothing.

Quickly she fanned through the remaining pages, but they were blank. That was all? She couldn't let it end there, she had to know! Were there other journals? Had Tansy thrown this one away after writing the horrible truth only to start another one when she could?

Cath jumped up and almost ran to the kitchen. Wenching open the door Jake had fixed, she flicked on the dim lights and hurried down the stairs, the door slamming behind her. She remembered where she'd found the first diary. Would there be more? Poor Tansy. Cath was almost as heartsick as Tansy must have been. She'd become involved with them, felt as if she knew Tansy and almost knew Jonathan. She'd so hoped he'd made it home for Christmas, instead, he had died. When? Where?

How had Tansy found out? How had she stood it?

Cath found the trunk and flung it open, rummaging around, but there were no journals.

She shut the lid and pulled down the box next to the trunk. Ripping off the tape holding it closed, she rummaged inside. Clothing. She felt through the stack to see if there were any books. None.

Tossing the box to one side she pulled down another. It almost fell from her hands it weighted so much. Opening it, Cath found the carton full of books. But a quick look and she knew there was no journal.

"Cath?" Jake called.

"I'm in the cellar," she yelled back, almost manic in her quest to find another journal. Tansy's story couldn't end with those brief words. What happened to her? Was she pregnant with Jonathan's child and didn't know it? Had she remarried, or remained a widow the rest of her life? Wasn't she a great-grandmother—therefore she had to have had a baby.

She pushed the heavy box aside, reaching for another.

"What are you doing?" Jake asked as he rounded the corner and saw her ripping into yet another carton.

"I'm searching for the blasted journal, what does it look like I'm doing?"

"Going through things like your life depended upon it."

She sat back on her heels and looked at him. "Jonathan died," she said sadly.

"Who—oh, the guy from Kings Mountain?"

She nodded, rubbing her chest. "I know it happened more than two hundred years ago, but honestly, I felt I got to know Tansy, she and I had a lot in common. Both our husbands gone on dangerous missions. Both of us lonely and alone. But I thought he'd come home. You came home. Instead the journal ended with 'Jonathan is dead.' I need to know what happened to Tansy."

Unexpectedly tears filled her eyes. She tried to blink them away, but the parallel was too strong. Tansy's husband had left never to return. That was the fear Cath had lived with for years.

What if Jake had been killed at one of the skirmishes he covered? Or at the earthquake center when another trembler shook?

Yet she was planning to send Jake away, never to return. How could she stand to have him out of her life forever? Was she certain that was the way she wanted things?

"Hey, honey, it's okay," Jake said, stepping over one of the boxes and squatting down beside her. He brushed away the tears that ran down her cheek. "Sad to know he died, but it's so long ago. You knew he was dead."

"But not like that. Not leaving Tansy behind. What happened to her? Oh, Jake, it's so unfair. People should fall in love and get married and live happily ever after. Not have one leave the other. I think she was only about twenty. They hadn't been married that long. What did she do for the rest of her life without Jonathan? Her love for him shone in every page she wrote." Cath couldn't help the tears, her heart ached for the couple of long ago. And for the couple of today. How had they come to this pass? She ached for love and family and a normal life with a husband safe at home each night.

Jake sat on the hard ground and pulled her into his lap, cuddling her as she cried. "We'll look and see what we can find. And if there's no other journal, we'll try the local historical society, or churchyard. We'll find out what happened to them."

"They're like us in a way," she said, burrowing closer, trying to feel safe, to have him wrap her in his arms tightly and never let her go. Her tears wet his shirt. Jake's heartbeat sounded beneath her ear, giving her comfort. His arms held her tightly, making her feel safe. The sadness was overwhelming. For Tansy and for herself. How had Tansy made it through? Cath didn't think she herself would want to go on if she knew Jake was no longer in the world.

Yet she was sending him out of her life.

Confused, hurt, sad, she didn't move. If she could stop time forever, it would be this very moment. Only, she wanted the ache in her heart to go away.

"It's getting cold, Cath. Let's go upstairs and sit by the fire," Jake said a little later when her sobs eased. "We'll have dinner and discuss how we can go about finding out about Tansy and her husband."

Cath didn't want to move, but she wasn't the one sitting on the hard-packed dirt floor. She pushed away and wiped her cheeks. Reluctantly standing, she surveyed the boxes and trunks stacked everywhere.

"I thought maybe Tansy started a fresh journal, one that didn't hold the bad memories the one I was reading did. She may never have written another word. I don't know. It was pure chance that I found that one."

Jake rose and looked around. "It could take a month to go through every box in this space. And, as you say, she may not have started another one. Let's try other means first."

Cath nodded. "If we can't find anything, I'll come back this summer and go through every single container in the cellar. I need to know what happened."

She needed to know that Tansy had moved on, found happiness and lived to be a grandmother who loved her family. That was the ending Cath wanted for Tansy—and for herself. She wanted some assurance that when Jake left, she'd be able to go on and find the family she so yearned for. She didn't want regrets or second thoughts. She didn't want to spend the rest of her life alone.

"Did your aunt do a family tree?" Jake asked when they went upstairs. "Maybe Tansy and Jonathan were on it and you'd have some indication of what happened."

"I don't know if she did or not. She talked about the family a lot when I visited as a young child. But not so much after I was grown. I think she felt she had told me all there was. I wish I had paid better attention. I don't remember hearing about a Tansy, though. It's an unusual name, I think I'd remember."

When they reached the living room, Jake added logs to the fire. The wood they'd brought in was dry and caught quickly. The room was noticeably warmer than the cellar. The lights on the tree seemed to grow brighter as the daylight faded into night. The snow continued, but the wind had died down.

"This beats the Middle East," he said, sitting on the sofa, and reaching for Cath's hand, lacing their fingers, resting their linked hands on his leg.

Slowly she leaned toward him, resting against his arm, her head on his shoulder. She still looked sad. He wished she'd smile, or laugh, or even get angry with him. He hated seeing her so unhappy.

Slowly she turned to look at him. "I should have made you welcome when you arrived. I'm sorry, Jake. I was just so set on ending our marriage, I didn't think about how you must have pulled some strings or something to get the time off. I'd much rather you be here than the Middle East. You could have been killed and never come home—just like Jonathan." Tears shimmered in her eyes again.

"No, Cath. I'd always come home to you." He had a sudden urge to give her the necklace, but held back. It would wait until tomorrow. Maybe it would cheer her up. Once he cleaned it, maybe the letters would reveal to whom it belonged. Wouldn't it be serendipity if it had once been Tansy's. Unlikely, however. The box was not from the 1700s. Probably someone had used it as a treasure box, hid it and forgot about it.

"This is a house made for a family, with lots of children," Cath said, gazing into the fire. "I hope Tansy found someone else to love, to share the farm with. Do you think she did?"

Jake couldn't get too worked up over a couple who had been dead for almost two hundred years, but he could see Cath was truly upset by her discovery. What could he do to take her mind away from it?

"I'm sure we'll find out. It may take a bit of time, but we'll find the answer. We can't do anything until after Christmas."

"I know. And it's probably silly, but I thought for sure I was going to read that Jonathan showed up in time for Christmas. I was counting on it," Cath said sadly.

His wife liked happy endings. He only wished she saw one for them.

Dinner was easily prepared and quickly eaten. Cath had little to say. Jake didn't push her. But he did watch her, conscious of the comments she'd made earlier about them not knowing each other well. They'd been married for six years, but he would never have expected this reaction to reading a two-hundred-year-old diary. He'd picked it up and scanned the last few pages. The death announcement was stark. Maybe seeing it written down had been the final straw for the young widow.

Or maybe she'd gone on to write a dozen more journals and they'd been lost or scattered over the years. He hoped they'd be able to find something out at the local historical society. Williamsburg prided itself on its history, surely the society would have information.

When they'd finished, Cath put a small plate of cookies on the table. "I should take some to Mrs. Watson, don't you think? If they hadn't come over today, who knows how long we'd have been stuck in the cellar."

"Take them tomorrow. It's pitch-black outside and treacherous to boot with the snow."

"Actually that'd be better. Tansy mentioned in her journal how they visited neighbors and friends on Christmas day. We'll be following an old tradition."

Jake could think of a new tradition he'd like to start. He rose and began to clear the dishes. Washing up took very little time. When they were finished, Cath looked at a loss.

Suggesting they go back to the living room, Jake found the Christmas records and put them on.

"Dance with me, sweetheart," he said, drawing her into his arms.

For a long time they danced to Christmas carols. She was sweet and soft in his arms. She made no move to end their closeness. Feeling bold, Jake began to give her soft kisses—first on her hair, then her forehead, moving down to her cheeks, and then capturing her mouth.

Cath sighed softly and encircled his neck, kissing him back.

"Come spend the night with me, Cath," he said softly.

She pulled back and gazed up into his eyes, hers soft and dreamy.

"I love you, Jake," she said.

Taking time to bank the fire, turn off the Christmas lights and shut off the record player, Jake leashed his impatience. He wanted to make love to her right then and there, but he wasn't some teenager unable to control himself. In bed, all night long, was better.

Hoping she wouldn't have second thoughts, he raced through the tasks and then walked with her up the stairs, fearing every step she'd change her mind.

"We only have the present," Cath said. "No one can see into the future. Would Jonathan not have gone to fight if he'd known he'd be killed?

Would Tansy have married him if she'd known they'd have such a short life together?"

"Hush, Cath. It's in the past. Didn't the journal say they were happy?"

"Tansy missed him so much. I knew how she felt."

"I'm home now, sweetheart." Jake drew her into his arms and kissed her again. She responded almost feverishly. He started to ask where, but decided for the bed he knew was large enough for both of them. The door to his bedroom stood open. It was cooler inside without the warmth of the fire from living room. But he had no doubt they'd warm up quickly.

Slowly they moved toward the bed, hands touching, lips kissing, the soft sighs and rustling of clothing being shed the only sound in the silent night.

The sheets were cool but momentarily. He eased her down and followed quickly.

"Oh, Jake, I love you," Cath said, reaching eagerly for him.

CHAPTER EIGHT

HAD last night been a mistake? Slowly coming awake in the still dark morning, Cath took stock. She was wrapped in her husband's arms. She felt cherished and well loved, but confused. She'd clung to Jake during the night, afraid of losing him as Tansy had lost Jonathan. Yet hadn't she considered all the changes she needed to make?

Being with Jake clouded the issue. She had tried to turn him away that first night. If he'd gone, things would be different. But he'd refused. Now they'd made love again and she had to admit how much she loved her husband. Together she felt whole, as if some missing part had been restored.

Frowning, she wished last night had never happened. It would be doubly hard to bid him goodbye now. She'd psyched herself up and all her arguments had fled like the wind when he kissed her. Would this change the dynamics of their marriage? Would he finally realize how much being together meant to her? She could counter all his objections, if he'd only give them a chance. They'd make a wonderful family, she knew it.

Cath slowly slipped out of bed, snatching up her clothes and heading for the bathroom. Time to get up and dressed and start breakfast. And think about a different future than she'd planned when she arrived at the old house a few days ago.

When she left the bathroom a little while later, Jake was leaning against the wall of the hall, wearing jeans and a loose shirt. He smiled when he saw her, leaning over to kiss her.

"Good morning. Why did you get up so early?"

"I wanted to start breakfast," she said. It sounded like a poor excuse. She wasn't brave enough to tell him how confused she was. He'd pounce on her uncertainty and get concessions from her before she knew what she was saying.

She needed to be careful, and make sure she knew what she was doing with her future.

"Make a big one, I've worked up an appetite." He kissed her again, then stepped around her and entered the bathroom.

Cath stood still for a few moments, relishing the embrace, fleeting though it had been. Her heart raced, her skin felt warm. For two cents, she'd turn and join Jake in the shower.

"Which would be totally dumb," she told herself. Putting yesterday's clothes in the laundry basket in her room, she headed downstairs. She went into the living room and turned on the lights. The sky was lightening, but remained overcast. It had stopped snowing with more than eight inches on the ground.

When she leaned over to plug in the tree lights, Cath saw two wrapped boxes, one larger than the other. She realized with a pang it was Christmas morning and she had not gotten Jake a Christmas gift! As his work could take him anywhere around the world at anytime, she'd had not bought anything due to the difficulty insuring the packages would reach him.

Yet there was the proof he hadn't forgotten her.

She tried to think of something she'd have that she could wrap and give him, but nothing came to mind. She'd have to confess she hadn't bought him anything. How sad would that be for Christmas?

Would he see her turning away similar to his mother? He'd lived with his mother's second family for nine years, but each year was more unhappy than the one before. He'd told Cath once how he'd felt like an outsider always looking in. And now she was going to make him feel like an outsider again. She'd bought presents for Abby and her family, even some of her friends. But nothing for her own husband.

What kind of woman was she?

Not that she would have minded yesterday or the day before. It would help cement her decision. But after last night, dare she hope things would be different? Maybe they could find common ground, start a family, find a way to have Jake work closer to home, or at least come home more frequently.

There was nothing she could do about it. She'd have to make it up to him in other ways.

Cath prepared a large breakfast of eggs, sausage, grits and toast, with orange juice and coffee for beverages. The last piece of toast popped up as Jake entered.

"My mouth is watering," he said, coming over to her and kissing her neck. "And not for the food."

She smiled and leaned against him for a moment, savoring the intimacy. She'd missed him when he was gone. She'd never get enough. "Eat, then we need to talk."

"Do you know how much I hate that phrase—we need to talk? It's never good," he said.

"What do you mean?" she asked as she served their plates and carried them to the table.

"It usually means a time to bring up bad news."

"Not this time. At least I don't think so. Sit down and eat."

"And then we'll talk, I know. So we remain silent during breakfast?"

She giggled and shook her head. "No." She sat and looked at him, biting her lip. "I'm sorry I need to tell you I didn't get you anything for Christmas. I didn't know you would be home."

"No problem. Actually the present I got you can be for both of us," he said easily.

"Oh." She gave a soft sigh of relief he didn't seem hurt. "Well, then, if you're not upset."

"No, Cath. After last night, I'm not at all upset."

She smiled in shy delight remembering.

"I have a ham I want to bake for dinner. I thought we could eat around one o'clock, if that suits you. Then later in the day we can take the cookies to Mrs. Watson."

Jake nodded.

His cell phone rang.

Cath groaned. "Not on Christmas!"

"It won't take long." He rose and left the room.

Despite last night, the scenario was familiar.

Nothing had changed. Cath finished her meal alone, watching as his grew cold.

She cleared her dish and ran water over it, setting it aside until he finished and she would wash all the dishes at one time. Taking her coffee, she headed for the living room, passing Jake who paced in front of the window in the dining room.

"Not what I want to hear, Sam," he said as she walked through.

She started a fire, settling back on the sofa and sipping her coffee. Even though it was Christmas, she could still look through other boxes in the cellar for another journal. Or even for the family history her aunt had accumulated. If the Historical Society was open in the morning, she'd try there as well. She hoped they weren't closed until after New Year.

Jake came in sometime later.

"Sorry about the call, Cath. It was important."

"Your breakfast got cold."

"Still delicious." He stood near the tree, hesitating.

That was unlike him. Cath always thought of him as charging right in. Was he about to tell her he was leaving?

Stooping, he swept up the two boxes and joined her on the sofa. "Two for you. Merry Christmas, Cath." He leaned over and kissed her gently.

Offering the larger box, Jake sat back to watch her open it. He hoped after last night she'd be glad to get the filmy nightie. He hadn't been able to resist when he'd seen it in the window of a shop in the London airport.

"Oh my goodness." Cath held up the sheer gown—it was pale eggshell-blue, with lace at the top and bottom, and lace shoulders. "It's beautiful."

"You'll be beautiful in it."

She looked at him with a hint of mischief in her eyes. "Let me guess, this is the one we'll both like."

He nodded, watching warily for any hint she was changing back into the freezing woman he'd found when he arrived. But she was as warm and close as she'd been last night.

"Thank you, Jake." She leaned over and gave him a sweet kiss.

"Want to model it now?" he suggested.

She laughed. "No. I know what will happen and I have to get dinner started before too long. The ham will take a while to bake."

"Later then, for sure."

She nodded, gently folding it and replacing it in the box.

"This isn't really from me," he said slowly, offering the smaller box. "I found these in the carriage house but thought they'd make a nice surprise."

She took the box, feeling something slide inside. Opening the paper, she lifted the lid.

"Oh." A gleaming gold locket lay on some tissue paper. Gently she lifted the necklace and held it in her hand. It was oval, about an inch in length. Initials had been engraved on the front with fancy curlicues.

"It's Tansy?" she asked, tracing a J and T. "Is this a locket from Tansy?"

"I thought of her when I found it. Jonathan and Tansy. It could be their initials, the engraving is so fancy it's hard to tell. Anyway, the locket looks old. Check out the fastener."

"It was in the carriage house?" Cath asked, lifting it gently, letting the delicate chain slip through her fingers as she gazed at the locket itself.

"In a metal box with some gold coin from the 1850s and a couple of Confederate coins. My guess is someone hid their treasure to keep it out of enemy hands and forgot it was there. Or maybe something happened to the person and no one ever knew what happened to the box. It wasn't buried very deep. I dislodge some dirt when I tried to move that carriage and found it."

"It couldn't have been Tansy, then. She would have died long before the Confederacy," Cath said. Slowly she opened the locket. A small curl of brown and black hair was tied in a faded ribbon, nestled in the tiny center of the locket.

"Or it was hers and passed down in your family," Jake suggested.

Cath touched the hair. "Whose, do you think?"

Jake looked at it for a moment. "Maybe both of them. There are two different colors there. Try it on."

Cath closed the locket, undid the fastener and presented her back to Jake, holding the ends in her hands.

"Fasten, please."

He brushed away her hair, fumbled with the unfamiliar connector, feeling her warmth radiating to his fingers. When it was hooked, he kissed the soft skin of her neck, moving around to her cheek as she turned to face him, ending at her mouth. It was a long time before Cath rose to check out the locket in the mirror.

Jake sat in the kitchen as Cath began preparing their dinner. She said she could manage everything when he offered to help, but would like the company. They still hadn't had that talk she'd mentioned earlier. Maybe he should open it up with his news.

"My call this morning was from Sam Miller, head of programming for the network," he began.

"And he wants you in some hot spot ASAP," she said without looking up.

"Actually I was getting feedback on my request for a stateside assignment."

She turned at that, staring at him in disbelief. "What?"

"I don't know if they can accommodate me. But I put in the request."

"You love your job."

"I'm not letting a job come between us. If it comes to the choice of my marriage or my job, I choose you."

Her face lit up. Jake felt his reaction like a kick. His desire flared. It was all he could do to keep from getting up and dragging her over to the table to make love with her again right then and there.

"That's wonderful. What would you do? Oh, Jake, this is the best present I could get." She wiped her hands on the towel and came over to give him a kiss. "You're really going to stay where it's safe? You'll be home a lot more, right?"

"Nothing's settled yet. But if they don't come through, I'll look for another network. I'm damn good at what I do. There have been other offers over the years. I'm sure I'll get something."

"There have?" She hadn't expected that, he could tell. Maybe he shouldn't be so forthcoming. But the comment she'd made about their not knowing each other rankled. He wanted to change that.

He'd never entertained moving from foreign reporting, so hadn't bothered to tell her when the offers had come before. Another mark against him. Cath was right, they weren't functioning as a married couple. That was going to change. If she'd forget her damn-fool idea of divorce, he'd do what he could to be the husband she wanted.

"One or two," he said casually.

She looked at him for a moment, then pushed away and went back to the food preparation.

Jake knew he'd blown it. He should have kept quiet about other offers. He spotted the cradle over to one side. Another topic he'd have to address sooner or later. Why had she fallen in love with that cradle? Maybe if he stayed home from now on, they could do enough together she'd forget having a baby.

"While the ham is baking, we could look again in the cellar for more journals," Cath suggested.

"If you want. This time we'll take flashlights," he said.

They spent most of the morning going through boxes near where Cath had found Tansy's journal. Nothing turned up. They moved deeper into the cellar, finding clothing from long ago. There were old shoes, the leather hardened and cracked. Another box had paper from early in the twentieth century.

"No sense in saving all this…it's all totally ruined," Cath murmured, as she rummaged through the mildewed pages.

"Clearing out this space is going to take longer

than we have now," Jake said. It looked to him as if the job would take a month of steady work.

"When you asked for a stateside assignment, does it mean as much travel as you've been doing?" she asked.

"There won't be as much, depending on the job."

"Any chance you could work from here? I still think this would be a great house to raise a family in. I could look this spring for a teaching job to start in the fall, give my notice where I am now at the end of the school year. That would give us the summer to sell the condo. Or we could keep it as a place to stay when we go to Washington. Or if you need to work there."

"Early yet to know what a new job would entail. Let's leave that up in the air for the present," he suggested. He didn't have a firm choice yet. But had been very clear when talking to Sam about what he wanted.

"I hate for this place to sit empty for so long."

"It's been empty for four months, another few

won't hurt it. We can come down every month for at least one weekend, to check on things."

"We could start fixing it up the way we want it," Cath chatted happily.

Jake felt impending doom at the direction of her thoughts. Just because he changed jobs didn't mean everything was changing.

She ripped the tape off another box and opened the flaps.

"I found them!" she called excitedly. "This box has several journals and I recognize her handwriting."

Jake joined Cath. She was fanning through different books, putting one down to pick up another. "I don't know the sequence, I wish she'd dated every first page just so I could put them in order. There are other journals here as well, different handwriting. Oh, this is so cool!"

"Let's take them upstairs and see if we can put them in some kind of order," he suggested. It was cramped in the narrow space between furniture and boxes.

"I hope she started writing after Jonathan died. The last one ended so abruptly."

"If not, maybe someone else wrote about her."

Jake carried the box up stairs and put it on the kitchen table. It was dusty and had cobwebs trailing from the base.

Cath wiped off the box, then opened it again and began to pull out the different books that housed thoughts of her ancestors.

The phone rang.

"Not again!" she exclaimed.

"It's yours, not mine," Jake said, pointing to the cell phone on the kitchen counter.

Cath dashed across to answer it.

"Hi, Abby, Merry Christmas!"

Jake continued to take out the books, opening each one to see if there were any dates. Some writers had dated each entry, but not the ones Tansy wrote. The dated ones he put in order. They were from the 1800s. The others had no dates. Maybe reading them would enable to determine approximate time frames.

"Things have changed for the best," Cath was saying. "I'll have lots to tell you when I get back. Are you having a good day? Yes, I want to talk to the kids. Was Jimmy thrilled with the bike?"

Jake turned slowly to watch his wife as she talked with Abby's children. She looked so happy. She loved being a teacher. She'd talked about it early in their marriage. She had that same glow now.

Jake turned back to the task at hand. Time enough to discuss a family later. For now, she was happy to find the journals.

Cath hung up and went to stand beside Jake. He explained the two piles, one with dates, one without. She skimmed the first few pages of each book in the undated pile. She'd gone through almost all of them, not finding one she thought was a continuation of Tansy's journal.

"Maybe she didn't write again," she said, setting yet another one aside and picking up a new one from the diminishing pile.

Jake was logging them into a file, with opening sentences for those that had no dates. "Wait, this is it. I recognize her handwriting. Listen to this," Cath said. "*I saw a robin today. It is the first sign of spring. And I was pleased to notice him. The winter was long and I still feel dark and chilled in my soul. I go to Jonathan's grave every day, but there is no comfort there. I've planted a rosebush and hope it grows. He loved roses.*

"*The farm is too much for me to handle alone now that planting season is upon us. I've hired a man to work the farm and invited my cousin Timothy and his wife to join me. I do not wish to live alone and they are young and full of life. I'm hoping to find some joy in living and maybe they will give me that.*" Cath looked up. "I wonder if this was written a few months after she learned of Jonathan's death. Sounds like it, doesn't it?"

Jake nodded. "Where is Jonathan buried?"

"I have no idea, maybe in the churchyard of

that old church out on the Williamsburg road. We could go look."

He glanced out the window. "When the weather improves."

"Sissy," she teased, going back to the journal.

He continued his task while she read silently.

"Jake," her voice sounded odd.

"What?" He looked up.

"She's writing about the gold locket Jonathan had given a neighbor to give to her on Christmas morning, one with their initials entwined. It was her most cherished possession. You were right, Jonathan had entwined a lock from both their heads to show they were joined forever," Cath said, rubbing the necklace. "Do you suppose he had a premonition he wouldn't be coming back?"

"He could have just thought he wouldn't be home in time for Christmas," Jake suggested.

Cath shivered with the knowledge the locket she was wearing was Tansy's. She'd suspected as much that morning, but this added to her belief.

As she read the words of the woman who had

died so long ago, she didn't find any mention of children. Tansy had not been pregnant with Jonathan's baby. Had she later remarried?

It was too soon after Jonathan's death for Tansy to be thinking along those lines. Yet Cath was impatient to find out what happened. She so hoped Tansy had found happiness—especially now when Cath found her own happiness. She couldn't believe Jake would change his career for her. For them. It showed how much he loved her. She'd be hard-pressed to give up her own job for him. Not that he asked her to—except to suggest she travel with him.

Did that mean he loved her more than she loved him? She felt odd with the idea. Why wouldn't she give up her career for the man she loved if he asked? Or even without being asked. Marriage was a two-way street. One partner couldn't make all the sacrifices. Had she been selfish in demanding he change? She wanted her husband home every night, but maybe it didn't have to mean in Washington.

The thought was almost too overwhelming. Had she expected more than she should have?

She'd been so sure this fall that leaving Jake was the right choice. Now that they'd spent some time together, she couldn't imagine not spending the rest of her life with him. And if he found a job in the U.S., it would mean they'd have a normal family life.

A lingering sadness filled her. Was it for Tansy? Cath was getting the happy ending denied Tansy.

She tried to shake off the melancholia. Her own life did not parallel Tansy's. Granted both husbands had been gone for an extended period of time, and both she and Tansy had missed them terribly and feared for their lives. But unlike Jonathan, Jake was home and safe. She didn't wish to delve beyond that right now.

After their early afternoon dinner, Cath wrapped the cookies to take to the neighbor. She dressed warmly and was ready before Jake.

"I don't see why we need to do this," he grumbled. "They probably have a ton of food and won't even eat the cookies."

"It's tradition," Cath said. "Tansy mentioned visiting friends and neighbors at Christmas. I want to start some new traditions as well. And if we move here, we'll want to be on good terms with our neighbors."

"A friendly hello as we drive out of the driveway would work," he said, donning his own light jacket.

"Aren't you cold in that?" she asked.

"If I stay out too long, yeah, I get cold. But the weather feels good after the heat I've lived in for the last few months. I have a heavier jacket at home, but didn't think to get it before starting out."

Cath should feel guilty her letter had sent him hurrying after her without the rest he needed, or the chance to get appropriate clothing. She should, but she didn't. His decisive move in following her showed her how much he cared. It meant all the more to her after last night. She was buoyed with hope for their future.

The walk to Pearl Watson's house was difficult. There was no sidewalk, so they walked across the yards. The snow hid any obstacles and made it difficult. Twice Cath slipped and would have fallen had Jake not caught her. She didn't know how Pearl had made it the other day. Of course the snow hadn't been as deep then.

The clouds parted and the sun shone, giving the snow a sparkling look as if a thousand diamonds glittered. It was almost too bright to see.

The visit was all Cath had hoped. Pearl had welcomed them warmly and thanked them for the cookies, which, luckily, Cath hadn't dropped when she'd slipped. A fire burned merrily in the fireplace and the living room was decorated to the nth degree with fresh pine and holly and many ornaments and figurines that Cath guessed Pearl had collected over the years. Jake gave every indication he enjoyed the visit, talking football and sports with Bart and com-

plimenting Pearl on her delicious mulled wine
and fruit cake.

Cath knew he was being overly polite—he
didn't like fruit cake. Still, she appreciated
his efforts.

They didn't stay long, but Cath enjoyed the
visit. It was fun, however, to return to their
home together, closing out the cold. They'd eat
dinner, she'd model the fancy new nightie and
knew exactly where they'd end up. She could
hardly wait.

CHAPTER NINE

As if deliberately building the tension, when they entered the house, Jake suggested they watch a movie on television. Christmas favorites were playing all week, and he thought one was starting in a few minutes.

"The only television is in your room," Cath pointed out.

He shrugged. "So we watch it there." His eyes gleamed, belying the casual tone of his voice.

Her heart skipped a beat.

"Want to take up some snacks?" she asked.

"Sure. Make it a light supper and later we can come down for dessert, if we want."

She sliced some ham, added an assortment of cheeses, heated the biscuits and cut a couple of apples. The warm cider would round off the makeshift meal, she decided.

She wasn't sure where Jake was while she was preparing their evening meal. She didn't hear any murmured conversation, so at least he wasn't on the phone. She spotted hers still on the counter and went to turn it off. Not that anyone was likely to call her, but just in case. She just wished she knew where his was, she'd turn it off as well.

And maybe chuck it out into the snow. Let him find it come spring!

Carrying the meal upstairs, she was surprised to find Jake had brought in a bunch of pillows, building a seating area for them on the double bed. A chenille afghan lay at the foot of the bed, to cover legs if they got cool watching the movie.

Soft lighting completed the ambiance. Cath smiled, feeling her anticipation rise another notch. Was he planning to watch TV or seduce his wife?

Jake switched on the set. The Christmas movie was just beginning. They watched the opening scenes of the familiar story while eating the light supper. Once they finished eating, Jake put his arm around her shoulder and pulled her close, snuggling her next to him as the action unfolded. Cath tried to concentrate on the characters of the old black and white movie, but she was too conscious of Jake pressed along the length of her. His scent filled the air. His warmth kept the coolness at bay. She glanced over but he seemed absorbed in the film. She reached out to take his hand and threaded her fingers through his, feeling his palm against hers. This was a moment she'd remember forever. The two of them together in perfect harmony.

"If we decide to move here, I think we should put a fireplace in this room," she said at one of the commercial breaks.

He looked at the outside wall where the chimney ran. "I suppose it could be fairly easily done, tapping into the existing chimney."

"And we'd build the dock you wanted. Get a small boat."

"Build a gazebo near the water, where we could sit on summer evenings," Jake said.

Cath took it as a very positive sign that Jake was participating in her daydreams of what she'd have her ideal house be. Maybe they would move here and make it reality.

To Cath's amazement, they made it through to the end of the movie. It was getting late. After making a big push to get her in bed since he arrived, she was a bit surprised he hadn't rushed her tonight.

"Ready for bed?" he asked.

"I guess."

"Try on the gown I brought," he suggested.

She nodded, rising. Away from him, she felt the coolness of the air. At least the bed would be warmed from their bodies when they got in again.

"Let me get the dishes done first." Was she deliberately tantalizing him by delaying? She smiled mischievously and gathered the plates.

Together they went downstairs. Cath put the dishes in the sink and rinsed them off while Jake turned off the Christmas tree lights and made sure the fire was contained.

He offered the box with the gown when she met him at the foot of the stairs.

"I'll change in the bathroom," she said breathlessly. She felt as shy as a new bride.

The gown fit perfectly, if a floating froth of sheer silk that flowed from her shoulders had any fit to it. The pale eggshell-blue was almost virginal. Excitement brought color to her cheeks. She brushed her hair until it gleamed, studying herself in the mirror. She looked like a bride.

Her heart tripping double time, she wished she had a wrap or something to cover her from the bathroom to the bedroom. Head held high, feeling feminine and sexy, she almost floated to the room they'd share tonight.

Jake had turned back the sheets and shed most of his clothes. He wore only the dark trousers. One bedside light gave soft illumination.

He looked at her when she entered and Cath heard his breath catch.

"You are so beautiful," he said, coming around the bed to meet her.

She was glad he thought so. Forgotten was the pain of the past, the long, lonely times. She had tonight; and their future. Cath was sublimely happy as she walked toward the man she loved.

"You're beautiful," he repeated as he reached out to touch her soft shoulders, slipping the lacy strap down a bit and bending to kiss her warm skin. "Gold and lace, you should always wear gold and lace," he said as he drew her into his arms.

The light had been extinguished, the covers drawn over them. Cath lay in blissful afterglow, reveling in being in Jake's arms. Her breathing had returned to normal and she felt safe and happy. This was how their marriage should have been all along. How it had been every time he'd returned home. She had lived in fear of his safety each time he left. His staying would make a world of difference. The one thing to make their lives complete would be a baby.

She suddenly realized they hadn't used any birth control, and Jake knew she wasn't on the pill. It was surely a sign he was ready to start their family, despite his words to the contrary. She smiled in secret glee. Maybe they'd make a baby that very night.

"Tell me about the job possibilities," she said, feeling warm and sleepy. She wanted to know more. How did he feel about making the change?

"I'm not sure what they'll have for me. Ideally I'd like a position that allows some analysis and then on-air reporting. On the other hand, it's the analysis part I like. I can do that without being the one to report it."

"Won't you miss the travel, seeing all those exotic places?"

"Exotic only if that's considered foreign. War zones and disaster areas aren't exactly the place of vacations. I've been doing this for twelve years, Cath. I might have done it for another twelve, but you're too important to me. Time to let others get the fame, and for me to settle down and come home each night to my wife."

She smiled, rubbing her fingertips against his strong chest.

Her decision had brought this about. She hoped he'd never regret giving up his way of life for hers. She'd do all she could to make him happy and glad he'd made this change.

"It could be that by next Christmas, we'll have someone else to share the holidays with," she said dreamily.

"Hmmm?"

"A baby."

She felt him tense. Her euphoric mood vanished in a heartbeat. She realized they really hadn't discussed anything of significance. He said he'd look for a stateside job. But there'd been no mention of how soon. And what if he couldn't find the one he liked? Suddenly Cath felt vulnerable and uncertain. They had not talked about starting a family. She'd told him she was ready. When would he be?

"What?" she asked, feeling constrained by his embrace instead of warmed by it. "If you get a job in the U.S., there's no reason we can't start our family. We're not getting any younger and I don't want to be old parents like mine were."

"Getting a job in the States is a long way from having a family. We need time to ourselves. Get to know each other all over again. I'm not sure I can live here. I might have to be in Atlanta or Washington or even New York. Too early to make firm plans until I know what I'll be doing."

"We've had time to ourselves. Six years' worth. And we will still have time for each other. It takes nine months to have a baby. And even after it's born, we'll make time for the two of us. I love you, Jake. I want to share in my life, share in yours. We'll always make time for us. But if you're home all the time, any arguments about having a baby disappear. It's time. Past time if you ask me."

"No."

"Hey, this is a two-way street. Are you telling

me you don't want kids? Ever?" Just when she thought things had turned for the best, he was throwing her a curve. What if Jake never wanted children? Her decision made this fall would have to stand. But after the last two nights, she wasn't sure she was strong enough to walk away from love.

"We can't have children, Cath," he said a long moment later.

"Just because your dad died young and you got a rotten deal with your stepfather doesn't mean you won't be a terrific father. I know you will be."

He brushed back her hair and kissed her. The darkness wasn't the cozy place it once had been. Cath wanted to see his expression. She wanted to rail against his stubborn stance. Why was he so adamant against having children? She knew he'd be a great father.

"Listen to what I'm saying, Cath. We can't have children."

"I don't see why you are so against it—"

"Dammit, *listen!* Cannot have children. Not won't, not delay. Can not."

She didn't understand. "Why not?"

He released her and sat up in the bed, drawing the sheets down with him. The sudden cool air against her skin didn't chill her as much as Jake's words.

She sat up, straining to see him in the dark.

"Dammit, what we have is good, Cath. We love each other. I'll stay with you, be with you. We'll do things like all married couples. We'll have a good life."

"As we would with children."

"I can't have children," he said heavily.

"What do you mean you can't have children?" she asked.

He sighed and got out of bed. She heard the sound of his jeans being pulled on. Afraid of what he would say next, she clutched the covers to her, trying to recapture the warmth.

"I cannot father a child," he said from the darkness.

"What?"

"I'm sterile. I had mumps when I was a teenager. There's no way I can ever father a child."

She stared at the place from which his voice came, picturing him in her mind, wishing the lights were on. The words echoed in her mind. *Sterile.*

Licking dry lips, she carefully asked, "How long have you known that?"

"Since I was seventeen and my younger sister gave me the mumps. The doctor had me tested afterward."

The words hit like a hammer. He'd wooed her and courted her and married her all the time knowing he could never have children. All these years she'd thought he was scarred by the experiences with his stepfather. That when they were ready, that when he was secure in her love, they'd start a family and he could finally experience how loving one could be. Instead she'd been kept in the dark. He'd always known they would never have a family.

"How could you not tell me, Jake? How could you marry me and not share this important fact? What were you thinking?" Her eyes were dry, the pain in her heart threatened to rip it apart. She was hurt beyond tears. He had to have known she would one day want children. All couples who married had children. At least all the ones she knew did. Yet he'd never given her a hint that they would never have a child together. Until tonight. Just when everything looked perfect, he'd hit her with this.

"There are lots of couples out there who have very happy lives without children," Jake said stiffly.

"Maybe if we'd built a solid marriage over the last six years, we'd have a chance. But this is more than I can deal with." Cath felt a part of herself die. "We've been married six years! You couldn't find a minute in all that time to tell me?"

"And have you say, sorry Charlie, I'm out of here? I've already had one woman turn on me, I didn't want another. We didn't discuss children at the onset. And over the years, we never talked about it. It was Sally's death that gave you the idea. Admit it. What we have is good, Cath. Don't turn your back on that!"

To her, having a family was fundamentally important. She was alone in the world except for friends, and for Jake. She wanted children and grandchildren and large family gatherings at holidays. She wanted love and quiet sharing times. Laughter and funny sayings of children to treasure. She yearned to share her life with offspring. Tell them about her parents and Aunt Sally, and even Tansy. To have continuity down through the ages.

But it was never going to happen. Jake had known that and not told her. In six years, he'd never shared that crucial fact.

She tried to absorb the magnitude of his revelation, but she was numb. She pushed aside the covers and rose. The nightie was somewhere on the floor, but she didn't even try to find it. It scarcely provided any covering. She went to the door and out into the hall and to her room. Closing the door, she locked it. Turning on the light, she quickly dressed in warm sweats and crawled into her bed. Her thoughts were in a jumble, but overriding them all was the knowledge that if she stayed with Jake Morgan, she would never become a mother. And he had known that all along.

Jake stood by the empty bed, listening to her walk down the hall, the closing of her door, the snick of the lock. He stared into the darkness, knowing his last hope had died.

It was only after several minutes, when he began to feel the cold, that he roused himself enough to get dressed. No point in getting back into that bed they'd shared. The memories would be more than he could deal with. He flipped on the light and found a sweatshirt. Dressing quickly, he pulled on socks and his shoes. Maybe a walk would help.

Hell, nothing was ever going to help.

He'd suspected this day might come. From the first moment she'd begun to talk about having children, he'd known he'd have to tell her. It had not seemed important before. She had children at school, he was gone a lot. But all fall she'd talked about it on the phone calls and their e-mail.

Why couldn't she have been some woman all caught up in her career who didn't want to have children? Or the favorite aunt of dozens of kids, so having her own wouldn't be as important.

Why couldn't he be enough?

He'd deliberately stayed away these last few months, hoping to delay the inevitable. It had worked, sort of. He'd squeezed a few more weeks out of his marriage. It would end for certain now. Getting a job in the States had nothing to do with it. Even if he were home every night, she'd never stay.

How ironic that he was finally willing to change and it would do no good.

He went downstairs. The outline of the

Christmas tree reminded him of the gift he'd given her. It had hurt a little that she had nothing for him. But she'd been coming from an entirely different direction. He'd not dwelt on it, but maybe he should have.

Yet, all he could remember was how beautiful she had been in the nightgown. At least he'd been given that.

Heading for the kitchen, Jake looked for the bottle of whiskey he'd had the other night. The way things were going, he was going to become good friends with alcohol.

He stopped and shook his head. He didn't need that crutch. The only thing it had accomplished the other night was to give him a headache in the morning.

He turned on the lights. It was two o'clock in the morning. Too dark to go for a walk, too early to be up, but he didn't feel a bit sleepy.

Mostly he felt lost.

Astonished, he sat down and gazed out of the dark window. He was a highly respected journalist. He had friends and acquaintances on three continents. He could write his own ticket for his career.

Yet without Cath, without their marriage, he felt adrift.

Like he'd felt when his father died. And when his mother had transferred her allegiance to her new husband virtually deserting her only son.

Anger took hold. If Cath only wanted a sperm donor, let her find one. If the bond they'd built over the years wasn't enough, so be it. He couldn't change that. He'd tried to rebuild their ties, to keep his marriage strong, but against this he had no defense.

Cath awoke late. She had been a long time going to sleep. The sun was shining, its glare reflecting off the snow, almost blinding in its brilliant light. Feeling groggy and out of sorts, she lay in bed wondering if she ever had to get up. Maybe she could just stay beneath the covers and not deal with life.

But she had things to do. Now more than ever she needed to decide if she was moving here, getting a divorce and moving on with her life.

Slow tears welled in her eyes. How could Jake have not told her? It spoke more to the flimsy strength of their marriage than anything. Granted, they had not discussed children before they married. Actually never discussed it at all. She'd said she wanted a baby this fall and he'd brushed it aside.

But she'd always thought they'd have children eventually. He had to know that.

Even if they didn't want children, wouldn't a husband have shared that major item of information with his wife?

Only if they had a strong marriage.

Which, obviously, they didn't.

The tears ran down the side of her face, wetting her pillow. It had been cruel of Jake to insist he stay for Christmas, for him to tell her he was returning to the States for good and then when her hopes were at their highest, to tell her the truth.

Her heart felt as if it were breaking. There would be no little boy with his daddy's dark hair. No little girl wanting to know the facts about everything. No children at all with Jake. Ever.

By the time Cath rose, she had a headache and was mildly hungry. She took a quick shower. Going downstairs, she was prepared to ask Jake to leave. If he refused, she'd leave. Abby would let her stay with her family until Cath could make other arrangements.

The house was silent. The Christmas tree wasn't lit, though its fragrance still filled the room. Cath barely glanced in. She went to the kitchen, gearing up to confront Jake. It, too, was empty.

Where was he? She looked out the window. There were prints in the snow, but nothing to tell her where he had gone. To the carriage house? On one of his walks? She didn't care.

She prepared a sandwich and ate it standing. Geared up to confront him, she felt let down he wasn't around.

Once she'd eaten, she went back upstairs,

carrying her cleaning supplies. There was one more bedroom to clean and the second floor would be taken care of. The work gave her something to do, and the exercise would burn off some of the anguish, she hoped.

The afternoon passed slowly. As she worked she made mental lists of things needed such as curtains for all bedrooms. The rugs in the rooms had been taken out and would require a thorough cleaning. She wanted a nightstand for the room she was working on, there wasn't one. Maybe she should paint the bedrooms. She could use a different color for each one.

For the time being, she'd keep the furniture. It was functional.

And she didn't need baby furniture.

She blinked back the tears. Nothing had changed from the day she left Washington. Granted for a short time she'd thought her world had changed. She'd thought she and Jake would have it all.

Instead she was back to square one—end the marriage and find a man who'd love her, stay with her and give her children.

When she finished the last bedroom, she vacuumed the hallway, and wiped down the bath.

Tomorrow, if she was still here, she'd begin on the ground floor.

Cath carried all the supplies downstairs. Leaving them in the dining room, she glanced at the stack of journals. She wasn't in the mood to read about Tansy and her life. It had an unhappy ending, just like Cath's.

She frowned. Not like hers. Jake was still alive and well. Tansy had lost her husband to death.

Cath swallowed. In comparison, she had so much. Tansy would have given anything to see her Jonathan again. Cath and Jake had spent several wonderful days together.

Going into the kitchen, Cath realized it was after four and she still hadn't seen or heard Jake today. Had he left? She raced back upstairs to check his room.

The bed was tumbled as it had been last night. Her new nightgown was in a pile on the floor. Jake's duffel bag was opened on a chair. Some of his things were strewn about. He hadn't left.

So where was he? she wondered as she went back to the kitchen. The cradle seemed to mock her, gleaming in the light. She should never have had Jake bring it up. Never cleaned it up and dreamed dreams as she envisioned a baby lying asleep in it. Their baby.

CHAPTER TEN

CATH put the ham in the oven to warm again and began to heat some vegetables. It was growing dark and she still hadn't seen nor heard from Jake. Where was he? Despite her heartache, she was growing concerned. She'd checked the carriage house and found an excuse to go next door to see if he was there. On her way back from Mrs. Watson's, she realized Jake's car was not in the driveway. Had he left without taking his things?

She stayed in the kitchen, not wanting to be reminded of decorating the tree by using the living room. Christmas was over.

She heard the car in the driveway. Anger flared again. She wanted to rail against him for keeping her in the dark for so long. Why hadn't he told her long ago?

Though she couldn't think when the appropriate time would be. Had she told him about her appendectomy? She thought so, but maybe not. Still, it wasn't the same thing. He'd known she wanted a baby this fall. The first time she'd brought up the subject would have been an appropriate time to tell her.

He hadn't because she would have left. He explained that.

Tears welled again. She dashed them away and began to calmly slice the ham when he entered the kitchen.

She heard the slap of papers on the table and turned.

"Your aunt did write a family history and turned a copy into the local library. They had a genealogy section with lots of information. All you want to know about Tansy and Jonathan is in there."

"You went to research Tansy and Jonathan?"

she asked in disbelief. He'd turned her world upside down and then gone off to do research?

"Wrapping up loose ends, Cath. I'll be leaving in the morning." He walked through to the dining room. A moment later she heard his step on the stairs.

No apology, no sign of regret. She stared at the thick stack of paper. He had flung them down and walked away. Tying up loose ends. She crossed to the table. Picking up the stack, she noticed several paper-clipped sections. One was a family history, another was the history of the house and a third looked like official documents from the county clerk's office. Jake had obviously spent all day locating this material. He knew she'd wished to know more, and had found what she wanted.

She sat at the table and began to read what her aunt Sally had written more than twenty years ago. When the buzzer sounded, it jarred her. She got up and turned off the stove and oven. Serving her plate, she went back to the table and picked up the pages. She'd read in her room.

Passing Jake's room, she hesitated by the closed door. What was there to say?

"Dinner's on the stove," she called, and turned for her room. She closed that door and sat in the chair near the window. Reading as she ate, and then continuing when she was finished, Cath was fascinated by the history her aunt had unearthed.

Saddened, too, to learn that Tansy had never remarried. She'd mourned her Jonathan all her life. And it had been a long one. She had died in the 1830s, at the age of ninety-two. She'd lived in the house Jonathan had built—the large house built for a family to grow in—until her death. It had been filled with love and laughter and children. Her cousin Timothy Williamson and his wife had had eleven children. And Tansy had helped raise every one.

Cath looked away from the history, wondering how much of what Tansy felt would be in the later journals. For a moment a shiver of apprehension coursed through her. What if she were more like Tansy than she wanted to admit?

What if she never found another man to love as she loved Jake? What if she mourned him all her life and lived to be in her nineties? She yearned for children, but not every woman who wanted a baby had one. Tansy had loved her cousin's children. How much must she have missed having her own with Jonathan?

The house had been in her family for years, but came down through Tansy's cousin, not Jonathan. Their last name had been White. It was Tansy's cousin Timothy who had been the first Williamson to live in the house.

Aunt Sally even wrote about the necklace, saying it had been lost during the Civil War, just as Jake had guessed.

Sally lamented the fact her nephew, Cath's father, had not wanted the old house. It should stay in the family. She hoped her grandniece would bring it back to life, and so she ended the history.

Cath could never sell it. Not after all this.

She might never fill it with children, but it was her heritage and she would hold on to it.

She didn't feel herself falling asleep, but woke with a stiff neck sometime later. It was almost 4:00 a.m.! She quickly dressed for bed and crawled into the cold sheets, going back to sleep. This time she dreamed she was an old woman, alone in a big house, with Tansy's necklace. She sat in front of a fireplace in the kitchen and lamented war.

When Cath awoke again, it was midmorning. She needed to talk to Jake before he left. She couldn't let things end like this.

He sat at the kitchen table, his duffel near the back door, when she entered a short time later. A hot cup of coffee held in his hand. He was reading one of the journals.

"Good morning," he said without looking up.

"Good morning. Ready to leave, I see," she said. Her heart raced. Sadness overwhelmed her. Six years of love and worry and loneliness and sparks of sheer joy crowded the memories of her mind. She saw a fabulously handsome, virile man sitting at her table, and her heart skipped a beat.

"It may be that I'm more like Tansy than I expected, though her blood doesn't run through my veins," she said, pulling out a chair and sitting before her knees gave way.

"No?" he asked.

"She never had children. She lived with her cousin and his wife and was auntie to their children. They were the ones to inherit when she died. She was Tansy White, not even a Williamson."

"You'll go on to have that family, Cath. Some smart guy will snap you up in no time and make sure you have a dozen kids if that's how many you want."

"Why didn't you tell me, Jake?" she asked.

"I figured you'd leave once you knew. I hoped against it, hoped you'd get enough of children at the school. I figured that's the way it'd play out if I ever had to tell you." He swallowed hard, studying her as if memorizing every feature. "Look at my mother. One child wasn't enough for her. She had to remarry and have three more.

Then her life was complete. Only somewhere along the way she forgot about that first child. Her second family became her focus. Things would have been different if my father had lived. But he didn't. And children became the over-ruling passion of my mother. When you first brought it up, I was stunned. For once in my life, I thought I was wanted for myself. Not for some genetic donation to create a baby. Never once in five years did you mention having children. Then suddenly, wham, it's the most important thing you can think of."

Cath blinked. She had never thought about his feeling that way. She knew about his family. He had shared that, and it had been hard for such a proud man to admit how left out he'd been as a child. He'd overcome a great deal to achieve all he had. She wouldn't for one second want to diminish that. Or consider him only a means to an end. She'd loved him, wanted his children as a part of that love.

She'd never considered this point of view. If

someone thought that of her, it would hurt. After all that Jake had gone through, she regretted his feeling that way. She'd never wanted to hurt him.

For a long moment all she heard was the sound of water dripping from the roof as the sun melted the snow. The fragrance of coffee would forever be tied to this conversation. She stared at him, not knowing what to say.

Jake broke eye contact first. He lifted his cup and drained it. "I'll be on my way in a little while. Thought I'd take one more walk along the river. I called Sam last night and canceled the request to stay stateside. I'll be heading for London in the morning. Have your attorney send the papers to the office and they'll be forwarded to me."

He rose, shrugged on his jacket and headed out.

Cath sat as still as a statue, fearing if she moved an inch, she'd shatter into a thousand pieces. How cruel her actions must seem. His announcement had caught her unaware, but that didn't mean she didn't love him. She didn't only want him as a sperm donor. She wanted her husband!

I thought I was wanted for myself. His words echoed in her mind.

All she could picture was the bewilderment a young boy must have felt when his father died. And again when his mother remarried and started a new family. Always on the outside, never feeling truly wanted.

Cath loved Jake. She had from the first time she'd met him. She hadn't been thinking about children back then, but about the most wonderful man in the world. A man who seemed equally taken with her. Would she have left him if he'd told her at the very beginning? She began to think she wouldn't have. In the beginning it had been just Cath and Jake. It was only lately that she yearned for more. Aunt Sally's death had changed things for her and she had only looked at her own selfish desire. Was it a woman thing, wanting a baby? She frowned. She did not want to be labeled a woman like his mother. She'd harbored uncharitable thoughts about the woman since she'd first heard about her. Today's revelation made her even more angry at his mother. She should have cherished and loved her first child. Had her goal been to have children just to have them, or to love and raise them?

What was hers?

She feared she was more like Tansy than she expected.

The truth was Cath had never looked at another man after she fell in love with Jake. Even thinking she was ending her marriage, she couldn't summon up a spark of interest in finding another man. Everyone would be compared with Jake. And found lacking.

But could she give up her dream of a family?

Two was a family.

She wanted more.

Sometimes in life people didn't get what they wanted. Aunt Sally hadn't. Her fiancé had been killed at Normandy and she'd never found another to love. Cath shivered.

Were there other women in her family who

were one-man women? What if she never found another man to love? Could she throw away what she had in the nebulous hope of finding love again?

She'd debated that in her mind all fall long. She thought she'd settled it. But seeing Jake changed everything.

"Cath!" A voice yelled from the yard.

She went to the door and opened it, stepping onto the back stoop.

Bart was running along the river, heading downstream, toward the McDonald yard.

"Bart?"

"Cath, get blankets and come a running. Jake fell into the river. I'm hoping to get him out at the dock."

She stood in shock for a moment—Jake had fallen into the river? He could freeze to death! She saw Pearl running from her house, two blankets in her arms.

"Cath, call for an ambulance. We couldn't get him out, the banks are too steep and it's so slippery with this slush," Pearl called, sliding as she ran after Bart.

Cath didn't hesitate, though she longed to cry out against the injustice of it all. He couldn't die! He'd been in wars and natural disasters, he couldn't die in her backyard. She whirled and went into action. As a teacher she'd been trained in emergency procedures. She called 9-1-1 and reported an accidental plunge into the James River. An ambulance was promised immediately. Cath flung on her jacket and scooped up the afghan from the sofa and dashed out the back door, running as fast as she could after Pearl and Bart. She could see them on the dock in the distance.

Over and over in her mind chanted the words, *wanted for myself.* She did want Jake for himself. For herself. *She loved Jake.* With a soul searing depth that frightened her. And gave meaning to her life. That would never change. How had she ever thought it would?

The slushy ground was slippery and sloppy.

The sunshine belied the danger beneath her feet. Melting snow made it almost impossible to keep from falling. Cath slipped and fell twice, soaking her jeans and scraping one palm. Keeping the afghan as dry as possible, each time she scrambled to her feet and kept going. Her heart raced, time seemed to drag by, each second an eternity. She had to get to Jake. Had to tell him he was all she wanted. He would be enough for her the rest of her days, if he only didn't die! God, don't let her end up like Tansy, losing the only man she loved!

The river water would be barely above freezing. How long would someone last in such cold water? Could he catch hold of the landing platform at the McDonald's dock? Was it still there? She hadn't used that since she was a teenager. Who knew what changes might have been made over the last ten years?

"Jake," she screamed, running as fast as the terrain permitted.

As she drew closer she could see Pearl on the

dock that jutted twenty feet into the river. Bart had jumped down to the landing platform. She caught her breath. Jake had been stopped by the platform, but she couldn't tell if he'd caught it or slammed into it by the river current. Bart was struggling to pull Jake from the water. In only a moment both men were lying on the landing. Jake was streaming water, soaking Bart.

Cath reached the dock and jumped down beside the two men. Bart sat up.

"You okay?" he asked, and gently pushed Jake to lie on his back.

His eyes were closed, his lips blue, but, thank God, he was breathing very faintly. A scrape near his hairline bled sluggishly.

Cath unfolded the afghan and wrapped it around him, snuggling closer to share her own body heat. He was soaking wet and freezing cold.

"Jake, say something. Are you all right?" she asked frantically.

"Here, take these blankets, too. He needs to get warm. That water is freezing," Pearl said, dropping down the blankets she held. "Are you dry enough, Bart, or do you need to wrap up, too?" she asked.

"I'm fine. My slacks are wet, but I'll be okay for a little while. Get Jake warm first," he said.

Cath was trying. She rubbed his face gently, feeling the chill of his skin against her palms. She feared her hands were getting too cold to help.

"Why doesn't he say something?" she asked, rubbing his hands, they felt like ice.

"I think he hit his head when he was trying to catch hold of the landing platform," Bart said. "He was doing okay until then. Good thing we saw him slip in. He could freeze to death in that water in just a few minutes."

They wrapped the blankets around him, but Jake made no move to help himself. Cath pressed herself against him. "He will be all right, won't he?" she asked. He was still breathing but was so still, and his lips remained blue.

The ambulance siren could be heard.

"I'll go tell them where we are," Pearl said, hurrying toward Cath's house.

"What happened?" Cath asked as she and Bart chafed his limbs, trying to warm Jake.

"He was walking along the bank, too close to the edge, hit a patch of slush and over the side he went. I ran out, he was holding on to a clump of grass at the water's edge, but we couldn't get him out. It's only about a three-foot drop, but the ground is so slippery with the slush. I couldn't get too near the edge, for fear of joining him."

Cath shuddered to think of both men in the water. Who would have fished them both out?

"He told me you spoke of a dock downstream, he said he'd try for that. Then he let go and drifted along the shore. I ran to tell Aunt Pearl and then headed for the dock. He was still lucid when he reached here, but wacked his head a moment later."

Cath held Jake tightly, saying everything she could to make him hold on.

"I love you, Jake. It doesn't matter about

anything else. We're a family, you and me. And that's enough. Hold on, love. Help is on the way."

Cath had never felt so helpless. Jake was her rock, her anchor. What if he didn't recover? What if he did but had changed his mind and wanted nothing to do with a woman like his mother who put so much emphasis on kids to the detriment of everything else?

"I'm sorry, Jake. So sorry. Come back to me. Don't be like Jonathan and leave forever. Stay with me. Grow old with me. Jake, please wake up!"

The paramedics hurried to the dock. In less time than Cath could imagine, they had Jake on a stretcher and were heading for the ambulance.

"We'll come to the hospital with you, dear," Pearl said, when Bart and Cath climbed up on the dock.

"Can't I go in the ambulance with him?" Cath asked.

One of the paramedics looked at Bart and shook his head.

Cath saw the sign and almost collapsed.

"I'm going!" she said. "And you're going to make sure my husband is fine!"

The ride to the hospital was a nightmare. Jake was so cold they broke out warming bags and packed them around him. He never regained consciousness. Once at the hospital, he was wheeled away and Cath was left to answer the questions of the admitting clerk.

Pearl and Bart arrived a short time later.

"How is he?" Pearl asked when they found Cath in the small waiting room.

"I haven't heard. He has to be all right!" She couldn't voice her fear that she'd left things too late. She would not become another Tansy. This family story would have a happy ending! At least she hoped so. She prayed for Jake's recovery, glad Pearl and Bart had come to be with her. She felt alone and afraid. What if Jake didn't recover?

She knew Tansy's anguish. How would she go on?

A half hour later a young intern came into the waiting room.

"Mrs. Morgan?" he called.

"Yes?" Cath jumped up and almost ran over to where he stood.

"It looks as if your husband's going to be fine. He's being taken to a room now. We want to keep him over night. He has a concussion and his body temperature is still well below normal. We're warming him up slowly and will monitor the concussion. You can see him in about fifteen minutes, room 307. But just for a moment. Rest and warmth are the best things for him now."

"Thank you." Cath burst into tears, feeling as if the weight of the world had been lifted. She had to see him, to make things right.

"We'll wait here for you, dear," Pearl said, settling back down in the uncomfortable seat.

"Take your time. We'll drive you home when you're ready to leave," Bart said, sitting beside his aunt.

Cath almost told them she'd never be ready to

leave, but knew the hospital probably wouldn't let her stay.

She found the room on the third floor. It was a semiprivate room, but only one bed was occupied. Jake was bundled in blankets, one hand lying on the sheet, the rest of him covered from neck to toes. He had his eyes closed, and a white bandage on his head.

She entered. Had he regained consciousness? "Jake?"

He opened his eyes and looked at her. Then he deliberately turned his head and closed his eyes, shutting her out completely.

"Oh, Jake, I'm so sorry," she said. Reaching out to take his hand, Cath was startled when he snatched it away, slipping it beneath the blanket, out of reach.

"You're going to be fine, the doctor said." She moved around the bed, but he merely turned his head the other way.

"Go home, Cath. There's nothing more to be said."

"Yes, there is. I was wrong. I'm sorry. I want our marriage to flourish."

"Get out."

"Jake, didn't you hear me?"

He looked at her then, his eyes bloodshot, his lips still faintly blue. "Did you hear me? Get out!"

"Not until you listen to me."

"Sorry, time for me to check vitals again," a nurse said in the doorway. "And I have some more warm blankets and a warm drink for you, Mr. Morgan."

"She was just leaving," Jake murmured, turning from Cath.

"I'll check on you later," Cath said tentatively.

"Don't bother. I'm only in here for observations. I'll be out in the morning."

"Then I'll come pick you up."

She left before he could say anything else. The nurse was already talking about seeing how much warmer he was.

Cath felt shell-shocked. He hadn't wanted to see her. She had apologized and he'd brushed it off.

She had to make him see she had a change of heart.

"How is he?" Pearl asked when Cath entered the waiting room.

"Cranky," she said, hoping it was the near death experience making him that way, not that she'd lost her last chance.

"Men do not make the best patients," Pearl said.

"I resent that," Bart said, rising. "Ready to go home?"

Cath nodded, feeling drained and tired. And immensely sad. Had she lost what she just realized was worth more than anything to her? How would she go on if Jake truly left?

When Bart dropped her off at the old house, he asked if she needed anything.

"Actually you could help me move something, if you would." She'd had enough time to think between the hospital and home. She knew what she was going to do. She was betting her future on it.

"Sure thing."

They moved the cradle back to the spot in the cellar where Cath had first found it. Without a second glance at it, she left it behind and followed Bart back to the kitchen.

"I appreciate your saving Jake, if I didn't say so before, I'm sorry. He's all I have."

"He might have saved himself if he hadn't hit his head. Glad I saw him slip, or he'd have been in a real mess."

Or dead. Cath shuddered.

"Let us know how he does," Pearl said, giving Cath a hug. "Want to come over to our place for supper tonight?"

"Thank you, but no. I have a lot to do before Jake gets home tomorrow. And if he calls, I want to be home." Cath thanked them both for their help and watched as they drove the short distance to Pearl's house.

Cath went to the living room and sank on the sofa, gazing at the ashes in the fireplace. She hoped they didn't reflect the state of her marriage.

For a long time she sat in thought. All the arguments she'd had during the fall rose, but were dismissed in light of the knowledge she now had. Finally she rose and went to find Jake's computer. With only a small search, she found what she was looking for. Using her cell phone, she called Sam Miller.

It took her a few minutes to get through to the man himself, but she patiently used Jake's name at every stage and refused to tell anyone else why she was calling.

When they were finished, she brought up the boxes for the ornaments and began to disassemble the Christmas tree.

CHAPTER ELEVEN

JAKE walked up the driveway. He'd had the cab drop him at the curb. The snow continued to melt. Some of the asphalt was visible now. His car needed to be cleared. He'd load his duffel and head out. He'd missed his flight, but once he got to a phone, he'd square things with Sam.

His head still ached. The doctor had told him it might for several weeks. He'd given him some pain pills, but Jake hadn't taken any. He was driving up to D.C. as soon as he got his things, no sense risking that by getting dopey on drugs.

When he reached the back door, he noticed the Christmas tree leaning against the house. It still looked fresh and vibrant. In only a few more days, however, the needles would begin to drop until it was merely brittle branches.

Sort of like he felt, he thought wryly.

Opening the door, he stepped into the kitchen. His duffel was still by the door, where he'd left it yesterday. Beside it sat two suitcases—Cath's.

He should grab his bag and leave. But he couldn't resist telling her goodbye. He'd acted like an idiot at the hospital. He hated her seeing him down and out. Things had been bad enough without that. He'd rather her remember him standing on his own two feet than helplessly shivering while trying to get warm.

Just then she breezed into the kitchen, carrying a heavy box.

"Jake! I was coming at ten to pick you up," she said, putting the box on the kitchen table. She ran over to him and hugged him. Involuntarily his arms came up around her and he buried his face in her sweet hair. Closing his eyes he focused on every impression, burning each into his memory. Her hair was soft and sweet and smelled like apple blossoms. Her body was feminine and curvy, molding with his. Her arms were tight around him, clinging like they'd never let go. Her voice was melodic, the prettiest he'd ever heard.

"I was so worried about you. I stopped back at the hospital last night, but you were asleep and the doctor said that was the best thing. They were checking you every couple of hours for the concussion, but it wasn't getting worse." She pulled back a little and looked up at him, her eyes full of concern.

"Should you be up and about so soon? How's your head?" she asked.

"It aches, but I was released with a clean bill of health. Just have to be careful and not bang it into anything."

She smiled, hugging him again.

"I came for my bag, Cath."

"Sure. Mine are ready. I did want to take the journals, though," she said, stepping away and moving back to the carton on the table. "Hold the door, will you?"

"What are you talking about?"

"Taking the journals?"

"No, that your bags are ready."

"I have to stop at the condo for my passport. And see about another set of clothes. Mostly I brought old things down here to do cleaning in."

"Where are you going?"

"Damascus," she said.

His eyes narrowed. Had the blow to the head addled his brains? What was she talking about?

"Damascus?"

She nodded. Picking up the carton, she carried it toward him. "Open the door for me, will you?"

He didn't budge.

"I'm going to Damascus," he said.

"I know, that's why I'm going," she said, standing in front of him with the heavy box.

"What are you talking about?"

"Get the door, this is heavy!"

He opened the door and followed her to her

car, opening the back door so she could slide the carton on the seat.

"I just need to put my suitcases in and get the lunch I fixed for us and I'm ready. I would have had this all done before ten, when I planned to go to the hospital to get you."

"Damascus," he repeated, closing the car door and studying her.

"I talked to Sam Miller yesterday and asked for the safest place closest to where you were going. He said Damascus. I can stay there and you can come home whenever you get a break."

Cath watched him close his eyes and shake his head, then heard him groan softly.

Anxious, she reached out to grab his arm.

"Are you sure you should be up?"

He opened his eyes and nodded slowly. "I just shouldn't be making sudden moves. Cath, you are not going to Damascus."

"I am. I'm going wherever you go."

"You're a teacher in Washington, not a nomad like me."

"I'm changing that. I love you, Jake. I knew it before I almost lost you yesterday, but that was a scare I never want to live through again. It showed me how precious our love is. And how fleeting it could be. I don't want to end up like Tansy, mourning you the rest of my life. Or even Aunt Sally."

"Aunt Sally?"

"She lost her love in the Second World War. She never found another. I can't take that risk when I already love the world's most fantastic man."

"I thought you wanted children."

"I thought I did, too. But what I wanted was *your children.* Since that isn't going to happen, then I'll drop the subject."

"Just like that?"

She hesitated only a moment feeling the pang at losing the dream. But compared with what she'd learned yesterday when she thought she might lose him, it was a minor price to pay, the loss of a dream. She smiled at him with all the love in her heart.

"Just like that. I love you, Jake. You and only you are who I want to be my family." She held her breath. She'd put everything on the line, faxing in her resignation, leaving her friends, to go with this man. What if he turned away like he had yesterday? It would be no more than she deserved, but more than she could bear.

He didn't move for a moment. Just when Cath thought she'd explode he reached for her, pulling her into a tight embrace. His mouth found hers and he kissed her long and hard.

"You don't have to go with me," he said a minute later. "I can still ask for a stateside assignment."

"I want to be with you. I'm tired of being alone. And I want you to know beyond anything how much I love you. You were willing to give up your career for me. I want to show you I'm willing to give up my job for you. I don't want anything to keep us apart."

"You love teaching."

"I do. I love you more. Besides, I can find a job teaching English in Damascus, I bet. I want you to know beyond a shadow of a doubt that you are all I need to make my life perfect."

He kissed her again, holding her like she was fragile crystal. Cath reveled in being in his arms, longing to remain there all her life. She'd readjust her plans for the future. Nothing was as important as being with this special man.

"You don't have to leave everything to show me you love me."

"I want to. I've never been to Damascus."

"I'll ask for a stateside assignment."

"After this one, but only if you want."

"I want. Maybe even something close enough we can stay in this house. It's your legacy from the past. Don't sell it, Cath. It's got a great history behind it."

For a fleeting moment Cath regretted there would be no children to leave it to when she and Jake no longer lived in it. But life was what it was. She'd already glimpsed what it would be like without Jake and what it could be with him. There was no hardship in that choice. She'd been fooling herself all autumn that she could leave. She could no more give him up than she could give up breathing.

"Whenever we're ready, we'll come back," she said. The future wasn't the one she'd thought to have, but with Jake it would always be more than enough.

EPILOGUE

JAKE paced the small room, stopping at the window, then turning to pace back to where Cath was sitting. The utilitarian furnishings were uncomfortable, how could she sit so calmly?

"How can you be so patient?" he asked. "Aren't you scared to death?"

She smiled and shook her head. "You've been shot at, almost drowned in the James River and had bricks fall on you from the earthquake last fall. What are you afraid of?"

"Messing up."

"You won't," she said with conviction.

"It's more than I can handle."

"It's not."

"You're sure?"

"Oh, yes. We'll make it—together." Laughter

filled her eyes. He frowned and turned to pace back to the window, staring over the bleak landscape. Snow had turned dirty along the side of the street. The black tree branches looked stark against the gray sky. More snow was predicted that night. He hoped the storm would hold off until they were gone.

They'd signed the last of the papers earlier that afternoon. Everything was set for their flight home. It was the waiting that was getting to him. And the uncertainty.

Jake turned and looked at his wife. She smiled at him, obviously amused at his behavior. For a moment he felt silly. He was a grown man, had faced dangers most men rarely even thought about. He couldn't believe Cath had given up everything to follow him. The last couple of years had been fantastic. They were closer than ever. They'd visited every capital in Europe, stopped in exotic locales around the Mediterranean. Theirs was a strong love that would sustain him through anything. Even this.

He hoped.

The door opened. Cath jumped to her feet. Slowly Jake turned, his heart pounding.

"Here they are," the woman said in heavily accented English. "Anna and Alexander. We call him Sasha as a baby name." Her uniform was gray, the apron she wore was white. Her eyes were kind.

The two-year-old girl stared at them, her blue eyes bright with wonder. Cath knelt near her and held out a dolly.

"Hello, Anna. I'm your new mommy," she said softly. Then carefully she reached out and pulled the child into her arms. "I'm so happy to see you today," she said, her voice breaking slightly. She closed her eyes for a moment, but not before Jake saw the tears.

Jake took a deep breath and stepped forward.

"Here you go," the woman said, handing the baby to Jake. He hesitated a moment, then took the seven-month-old boy. The baby's blue eyes stared up into Jake's. For a moment panic took hold, then sanity returned. He'd wanted to do this. For Cath, and for himself.

Now he was a father of two children, orphaned by the fighting in their home country, alone in the world except for him and Cath.

The baby's fist waved and Jake caught it, feeling the tiny fingers wrap around his thumb. He said the words he'd never expected to say.

"Hello, Sasha, I'm your daddy."

Already he felt the tendrils of love wrap around his heart. He looked at Cath and smiled. They had discussed the option of adoption shortly after they arrived in Damascus. Cath had a heart full of love to share, and he wanted to be right there with her. She was right, together they could do this.

They were flying home tonight—to spend Christmas at the house beside the James River. He had a yard to fence, a dock to build and two precious children to love and raise. Their legacy to the future.

"Ready, Daddy?" Cath asked, picking up Anna and carrying her over to Jake.

He leaned over and gave the little toddler a kiss on the cheek, then one for Cath.

"We're ready, Mommy, let's get our kids home."